The Scarred Governess of

A HISTORICAL REGENCY ROMANCE NOVEL

Sally Forbes

Table of Contents

Prologue

Winter, 1812

Rosalie Stewart sat at her father's bedside, watching his pale face as he slept.

"Oh, when will that darn physician arrive?" she whispered to herself, chewing on her lip.

That day was not the first that his condition had taken a downturn since he fell ill two months prior. It was the worst she had seen him, and it had happened in just a matter of minutes, right before her eyes. She prayed the doctor would arrive with medicine and help her father to feel better, so he could continue to fight his illness.

Rosalie looked outside, hoping to distract herself from her worry and frustration. But the cold winter day offered her nothing in the way of solace. Rather, the gray sky and heavy snowfall only added to her despair. On such days, it was impossible to believe that things would ever get better.

At long last, she heard a knock on the front door, sounding muffled through the closed door of her father's chambers. She quietly rose and slipped out of the room, hurrying to the door to usher the physician inside.

"Tell me a little about his new symptoms," the doctor said, giving her a warm smile as she led him back to her father's room.

"The only new symptom is a terrible wheezing in his chest," she said. "Apart from that, his fever has spiked drastically, unlike ever before, and it is resistant to my efforts to lower it. He is also having trouble communicating clearly with me again, but this time, he mostly just mumbles. And what I can hear is essentially nonsense."

The physician nodded, his eyes calculating. He remained silent until they reached Albert Stewart's sickbed.

"Good day, Mr. Stewart," the doctor said gently, just loud enough for the ill man to hear.

When her father did not stir right away, the physician looked at Rosalie gravely.

"Perhaps you should step outside while I conduct my examination," he said.

Rosalie opened her mouth to protest, but then she glanced at her father. The most important thing was getting him well. And if the physician believed he could best do that with her waiting outside, then she would do just that.

"Very well," she said. "I will be just here in the hallway. Please fetch me as soon as you have finished."

The doctor nodded again, giving her a silent, understanding smile. Rosalie stepped out of the room, closing the door behind her. *Please help my father,* she prayed silently, though she did not know quite to whom. Then, there was nothing but to wait, which Rosalie thought would claim her sanity.

When the physician emerged from her father's room, his face was tired and grim. Still, she held hope that he could offer her some good news.

"Were you able to help Father?" she asked.

The doctor looked at her, his eyes filling with sadness that was quickly felt in her heart.

"Miss Stewart," he said, in a voice as grave as his expression. "I am afraid that there is nothing more I can do for your father. The illness is claiming him, and fast. I have given him medicine to make him comfortable, but apart from that, he is beyond treatment."

Rosalie sobbed.

"No," she whispered. "Surely, there is something else that can be done. Could another doctor help us?"

The physician shook his head sadly.

"Your father lies on his deathbed, my dear," he said, giving her arm a gentle pat. "Even if another physician could come to you today, in this weather, I fear your father would not be alive to see him."

Rosalie closed her eyes, praying she would awaken from a bad dream. But when she opened them, the physician was still looking at her with heartbroken sympathy. She felt guilty for implying that he had not done his job with examining her father properly

"Thank you, doctor," she said. "Please, do not think I was questioning your skills. I just cannot believe that I am losing my father."

The doctor shook his head, giving her a warm smile.

"Not at all, Miss Stewart," he said. "I understand your sentiment perfectly. I am only sorry that I have had to give you such terrible news."

Rosalie wiped tears from her cheeks.

"You did all you could," she said. "And for that, I shall forever be grateful."

She reached into her dress pocket and pulled out her coin purse. She paid the physician, trying not to wince as she realized it was the last of the coin she had. Then, she walked him silently to the door, seeing that he got safely into his hackney, with all the snow that rested on the ground.

Once he was gone, she wiped her face with her handkerchief and went into her father's room. She tried to be brave, but the sight of her dying father tore her heart to bits.

Albert Stewart stirred when his daughter entered the room. He gave her a weak smile, and she felt more tears begin to fall.

"Come, sit with me, my darling daughter," he said, weakly motioning for her to come to him.

Rosalie obeyed, taking his outstretched hand in both of hers.

"You should rest, Father," she said, choking back sobs.

The dying merchant shook his head.

"The time for rest comes soon enough already," he said. "But now, I wish to say something very important to you."

Rosalie could not suppress the sob that escaped her throat. She knew her father was preparing to say goodbye to her, and she was devastated. But as much as it hurt, she could not bring herself to deny her father his dying words.

"Of course, Papa," she said, crying. "I will hear what you have to say."

Her father nodded, taking a slow, labored breath.

"I fear I have not told you this enough in the time we have had together," he said, a rattle beginning in his chest as he spoke. "But I wish to tell you now. You have always been the most special person I have ever known. And you always will be special, Rosie. I need you to promise me that, no matter what, you will always remember how special you are. You are smart, capable, and absolutely beautiful. You must not ever forget it, sweetheart. Please. . ."

He trailed off as breathing became more of a struggle for him.

Rosalie squeezed and patted his hand, sobbing uncontrollably. She would never dream of leaving her father to die alone, but watching it actually happen was breaking her heart to pieces.

"I promise, Papa," she said, ignoring the urge to argue with him. Now was not the time to tell him how much she disagreed with him, or how hideous she believed she really was.

Albert slowly regained some ability to speak, and he took another congested breath.

"Thank you," he said, motioning to his daughter's heart. "And one more thing, Rosie dear. You must also always stay true to yourself. There is nothing more important in life than that. Be true to yourself, and you will never feel any doubt."

Rosalie nodded, even though she did not quite understand what her father meant. She wanted to ask him, but he was fading fast, and she knew they were almost out of time. If she did not make the most of the time they had, she would not get to say goodbye to her father. That was something with which she could not live.

"I will, Papa," she said, wiping tears from her cheeks, only to have them replaced with more instantly. "I will do as you ask."

The merchant tried to nod, but his entire torso began to seize, and his breath came shortly and with difficulty.

"Papa, I love you," she said through her sobs. "Rest now. I will be here with you for as long as you need me."

Albert gasped, turning his head weakly to his daughter.

"I love you too, Rosie," he rattled. "Goodbye, darling."

"Goodbye, Papa," she whispered.

The man tensed in his bed, gripping Rosalie's hand tighter than he ever had before. Then, he relaxed, for the very last time, his breath escaping him with a final, vicious rattle. And then, silent stillness.

Rosalie sat and cried for half an hour. She knew she must summon the physician once more, but she was too bereft to move.

When at last she did, she quickly scribbled a note, to be delivered immediately. She could not bring herself to leave her father's side, even though he was no longer with her. Then, she waited, grateful for the numbness that claimed her as she did so.

The funeral was very small, attended only by a couple of her father's closest friends, whose names Rosalie was too depressed to remember. She thanked them for attending, and for their condolences, nonetheless. Her aunt was there, as well.

As she was her mother's sister, Rosalie had only met Grace a few times in her life. The last time she had seen her aunt was shortly before her father fell ill. She had always been kind to Rosalie, however, and she was glad she had come.

Rosalie was alone in the world. With her father's passing, she was an orphan, having lost her mother to a fever when she was just two years old. And even though she was eighteen now and of an age to care for herself, she was hardly prepared to do so.

She was well aware that her father's death immediately ceased the income flow, and that there were many debts outstanding, which the merchant had been still trying to pay off before he died. Sadly, she had not been left the skills to handle such financial affairs—or the money to do it.

When the funeral ended, Grace stayed behind to console her niece. Rosalie cried for a time, feeling great comfort from her aunt's arm around her. She imagined it was like the embrace of a loving mother, which only made her cry even more. She had never really known her mother, as she was far too young to remember her when the fever claimed her. But in this time of need, she wished her mother was still alive.

"What will you do now, darling?" Grace asked, stroking her hair.

Rosalie sighed.

"I do not know," she admitted. "The last of father's wealth was used to pay for the funeral, pay off his creditors, and settle the medical bills over the last month. He always arranged to pay rent six months in advance, but that will expire in less than two months. And there is not enough food in the house to last that long, anyway. I suppose I must spend some time thinking about what to do in the coming days. I am sure I will come up with something."

Grace looked at her niece thoughtfully. Rosalie tried to sound calm, but she was well and truly distressed. She had no idea how she would take care of herself, even if she took months to figure it out. But she was eighteen years of age. It was her responsibility to handle her father's affairs and look after herself. Even if she did not yet know how.

"No," she said simply, rising and reaching for Rosalie's hands. "That simply will not do, my dear."

Rosalie frowned, taking her aunt's hands and allowing herself to be pulled to her feet.

"What else can I do?" she asked, perplexed.

Grace wiped away tears from Rosalie's cheeks and smiled fondly. Rosalie imagined that her mother had looked much like Aunt Grace, and she at last felt a small bit of true comfort.

"I hope this was not presumptuous of me," Aunt Grace said, suddenly looking very nervous, "but after I got the news that your father had died, I spoke with the Earl and Countess of Winsdale. I am housekeeper for them, and I heard from the other servants that they are seeking a governess. So, I asked if they would consider hiring you, after the funeral, of course, should you need a job to make ends meet. And they were happy to oblige. They have held off on interviewing any other governesses until you speak to them. If, that is, you choose to take the position."

Rosalie gasped, throwing herself into her aunt's arms.

"Presumptuous?" she exclaimed. "Aunt, I believe you have just saved my life."

Chapter One

Early Summer, 1818

"Oh, dear," Rosalie murmured to herself, scouring yet another newspaper for ads from people seeking a governess, and once more coming up with nothing. "What will I ever do with myself?"

She exhaled through pursed lips, blowing a strand of her wispy blonde tresses out of her eyes. The gesture proved useless, and she tucked it behind her ear with frustration. Then, she massaged her temples, pushing aside the paper and closing her eyes to give them a rest, before her headache could worsen.

She could not believe her terrible luck. She had served the Earl and Countess of Winsdale as the governess for their children since her father died, and both she and her employers had been happy. But, as children do, her charges had grown up, and now, they no longer needed a governess.

When the countess had kindly offered to allow her to stay at their manor until she found other employment, she had been thrilled. Surely, a young woman with her experience, having worked so long for such a reputable couple, would not be out of work for very long.

How wrong she had been. Weeks after Lord and Lady Winsdale had terminated her employment, she was still no closer to finding a new job than she had been on the day when they released her from her duties.

The earl and countess had been endlessly patient, and they showed no signs of growing frustrated with her lingering presence. But Rosalie knew their understanding could not last forever. They could not carry her financially for the rest of her life, and she was dangerously close to the end of the severance pay they had given her.

The employment agency had been of no help, either. She had gone in there weeks ago, optimistic, and confident she would be able to find work right away. Even when they had rejected her the first time, she was not disheartened. She had been sure that new employment would eventuate, and that she had plenty of time to wait.

But now, as she prepared to travel to the agency for a fifth time, she no longer felt confident or hopeful. In fact, she felt humiliated and dejected, and properly concerned for her future. She had hidden her lack of success from her Aunt Grace, but it would not be much longer before she would begin to ask questions.

What would she say to her aunt, who had been so kind as to get her the governess position with the earl and countess? How would she take care of herself if she did not find work very soon?

With one last bout of determination, she looked at herself in the mirror. Her only option, should she fail at finding employment, was to end up in the poorhouse, begging on the streets for alms. Her father had raised her better than that, and she refused to allow that fate to befall her. Gathering up her courage and a hollow smile, she tidied her hair and then departed for the employment agency once more.

She tried to remain hopeful and optimistic as she entered the agency's lobby door. But when the smile on the clerk's face dissolved as soon as he made eye contact with her, she felt her cheeks flush with shame. Still, she had come this far, all over again, and she was determined to hear the answer aloud.

"Excuse me, sir," she said, curtseying politely. "I am sure you remember me from last week…"

"I do," the curt man said, cutting her off. "And from the past several weeks previous, as well."

Rosalie's blush deepened, and she felt her eyes begin to sting.

"Yes, of course," she said, clearing her throat. "Well, I just came to see if there have been any job openings for my preferred position yet."

The man stared at her with disgust for several long, uncomfortable moments. Rosalie was instantly sure he was being unpleasant on purpose, but she tried to hold his gaze with a modicum of casual confidence. When the man sighed, she held her breath, hoping he was just in a foul mood that had nothing to do with her, and that maybe, he would have good news for her.

"No," he said. "There is still nothing for a woman like you, Miss Stewart."

Rosalie's frustration began to take the form of indignance as she considered the man's words. *A woman like me?* she thought, considering her next words. But the realization of why the man was looking at her with such abhorrence hit her like a racing horse, and she had to force herself to curtsey once more.

"Thank you, sir," she said, turning away from the man. She walked out of the agency slowly and with her head held high, but her cheeks were soaked with tears before she reached the carriage. Her humiliation was second in her mind, however.

Once again, she had been rejected by the agency for employment. Deep down, she knew they were not matching her with opportunities because of her appearance. But the reason was ultimately irrelevant. The result was still that she had no work, and she would have to return home and deliver the same disappointing news yet again.

Distraught, she cried all the way back to Winsdale Manor. There was no getting around telling the kind countess or her aunt of her recent failure. She had long since given up on praying for miracles, as she found that no such prayers were ever answered. Instead, she prayed to become invisible to everyone at the manor until she could face them. Even if that time never came.

With her head down and her cheeks burning, Rosalie slipped back inside the house as quietly as she could. With a little luck, everyone in the household would be busy with other activities and miss her arrival. She was just beginning to think that luck favored her at last when she turned a corner down the hallway and nearly ran straight into her aunt.

"There you are, darling," Grace said, taking her hand and tugging it. "The countess asked me to find you, so she can speak to you straight away."

Rosalie groaned, covering her face with her hands.

"Oh, dear," she said, shaking her head. "Could she wait until I can freshen up a little?"

Grace put her hands on her niece's shoulders.

"She requested that I send you to her as soon as I saw you," she said. "What is wrong, darling?"

Rosalie considered telling her aunt about her most recent rejection for work, but she hesitated.

"I suppose I must wait until later to tell you, if the countess is adamant on seeing me now," she said.

Her aunt embraced her briefly, giving Rosalie a small measure of comfort.

"All right, dear," she said. "I do hope that what the countess has to say will be good news to you."

Rosalie pulled away and looked at her aunt with confusion. She was only met with a mysterious wink before the elder woman ushered her to the drawing room.

Rosalie collected herself, then entered the room. Right away, she saw that the countess had company. A very regal lady stood beside Lady Winsdale, and Rosalie instantly felt self-conscious.

"Oh, please forgive me," she said, bowing her head. "I can come back later and give you and your guest some privacy."

The countess laughed, beckoning Rosalie to approach.

"No, dear," she said, her voice as warm as it ever was. "I summoned you because I would like you to meet Dorothy Livinwood, the Dowager Duchess of Livinwood."

Rosalie squirmed, cursing the heavens for not letting her slip away to her quarters unseen. She was terribly ill-prepared for meeting anyone at that moment, let alone more of London's nobility. Still, Lady Windsale was as yet her mistress, and since she was living in the manor for nothing, she knew she must oblige.

"It is a pleasure, Lady Livinwood," she said, dipping into a curtsey. "I am Rosalie Stewart."

The duchess smiled, nodding her head at Rosalie's greeting.

"Likewise, Miss Stewart," she said.

Rosalie blushed, noting that the new woman's voice sounded as warm as her expression appeared. She tried to relax, wondering why she had been summoned to such a meeting.

Lady Winsdale motioned for Rosalie to take a seat near the two women. Rosalie's heart leapt into her throat, but she obeyed her former mistress. She sat down, trying her best to hide the blemished side of her face, even though the duchess had undoubtedly already seen it.

"I am at your service," she said bashfully, not sure if she was talking to her former employer or the new noblewoman standing before her. She glanced nervously at the women, hoping one of them would end her misery soon, so she could go to her room and recover from the day.

"Miss Stewart," the duchess said softly. "The countess tells me that you are seeking employment. She also assures me that you are the best governess she has ever encountered."

Rosalie blushed, unsure of what to say. Such praise was still unfamiliar to her, especially coming from a stranger. But she did not wish to be offensive. She simply curtseyed once again.

"That is kind of her," she said. "I have done my best to please Lord and Lady Winsdale, these past few years."

The duchess seemed pleased with her response.

"It sounds as though you certainly have," she said. "Which is why I would like to hire you to be my granddaughter's governess."

Rosalie felt her knees try to buckle with relief. Her mouth quivered, and she had to bite her cheeks to stifle a sob. She fumbled quickly for her words, as this was hardly an opportunity she could let slip through her fingers.

"When would you need me to start?" she asked, failing to sound anything less than excited and emotional.

The duchess smiled warmly.

"Are three days from now suitable for you?" she asked. "My son, granddaughter, and I will be taking up residence in our countryside home for the summer. You would need to arrive there the evening before, so the staff can help you get acquainted with the manor. And then, you will meet my granddaughter and begin lessons with her on the third day."

It was all Rosalie could do not to cry. It felt as though, for the second time since her father's death, her prayers had been answered. And for the second time, it was the Countess Winsdale who had answered them. She owed the woman a wealth of gratitude, and she would begin by taking the job she had so graciously placed before her.

"Yes, my lady," Rosalie said, grinning. "That is perfect for me. I shall arrive at your country home in two days."

Chapter Two

Cedric, Duke of Livinwood, dismissed his valet once the man had helped him to dress. He smiled at his reflection, his blue eyes glittering with the joy of being able to spend time away from London at his countryseat. Quickly, he ran his comb through his light brown locks, straightening his shirt and coat before heading downstairs to join his mother and sister for breakfast.

He made a mental note to ask his mother a very important question as he made his way to the main dining hall. He doubted the dowager duchess would have an answer for him, but it could never hurt to ask.

"Good morning, dear," his mother said, coming to greet him as he entered the room.

"Good morning, Mother," he said, kissing her cheek and escorting her back to her seat beside his sister. He patted her gently on the head as he passed her, smiling fondly when she looked up and poked out her tongue at him.

"I am not a child any longer, Cedric," she said, trying to keep a straight expression of indignance, despite the smile threatening to break through it.

"Oh, Olivia, dear," he said, grinning. "Until you are older than me, you will always be my little sister."

His younger sister made another face, one which quickly gave way to smugness.

"Call me *little* all you wish," she said, "but I am a young woman of nineteen, in my second London Season. I bet that when I am married, you will no longer call me a child."

Cedric chuckled as he helped himself to the breakfast spread before him.

"Of course not, Sister," he said. "I shall then call you a baby."

Olivia gasped, bursting into a fit of giggles.

"You are incorrigible, Brother," she said, shaking her head.

The dowager duchess smiled indulgently at her adult children, waiting for them to fall silent. Cedric turned his attention to her, sensing she had something she wished to say to him.

"Cedric, darling," she said when he and Olivia had quieted, "I want to let you know that I paid a visit to Lady Winsdale two days ago. I said nothing because I wanted to see how things would turn out before I spoke about it. But you will be happy to know that I have found a new governess for our little Sophia."

Cedric choked on his eggs, startled by the duchess's words. His mother had answered the question he'd intended to ask, but he had not expected the news she had delivered.

"What?" he asked, swallowing hard to dislodge the trapped food from his throat.

His mother smiled brightly and nodded.

"Yes, my dear," she said. "It turns out that their former governess is seeking employment. And I believe that this time, things will work out beautifully."

Cedric's mood darkened. He appreciated his mother's efforts, but he sincerely doubted that "things would work out this time" at all. After all, he and his eight-year-old daughter had been through many governesses, all of whom had vanished because of their discomfort with Sophia's eyes.

It seemed that none of them could get past the fact that one of them was blue, and the other was brown. One old shrew of a woman had even had the gall to call the little girl 'the spawn of the devil,' which had upset Sophia for weeks.

"Who is she?" he asked, trying to mask his skepticism. "Does she know of our plans to go to our countryseat?"

His mother nodded.

"Her name is Rosalie Stewart," she said, clearly excited. "And yes, she is aware we will be leaving shortly for the country. She is perfectly agreeable to leaving London and coming to reside with us there."

Olivia gasped loudly, grabbing the attention of both her mother and her brother.

"Surely, you are not serious," she asked, her face twisted in horrified disapproval. "You must have been mistaken about the woman's name, Mother."

The countess looked at her daughter, perplexed.

"I am not at all mistaken, dear," she said. "I spoke with both Miss Stewart and Lady Winsdale, with whom she was most recently employed. She is a lovely young woman, and I believe she is perfect for our dear Sophia."

Olivia snickered.

"Lovely and perfect, she certainly is not," she said. "There is much gossip within the *ton* about her beastly appearance."

Cedric bit his cheek, not wishing to make a scene over his sister's remark. Their mother was less tolerant, however.

"You should be ashamed of yourself, Olivia," she said. "That you could say something so cruel about someone's appearance is abhorrent. I will not have you speaking about our new governess in such a way."

Cedric nodded, giving his mother a grateful glance. He tried to keep his offense at his sister's remarks in check as he addressed her.

"You really should not allow yourself to get so caught up in the *ton's* gossip," he said, giving her a meaningful look. "London's high society is constantly looking for something that offends its delicate sensibilities. A person's appearance should be the least of everyone's concern."

Olivia shook her head firmly, rising to her feet and stomping.

"You have no idea of the scandal you will bring to our family name by having such a ghastly woman working in your employ," she hissed.

Cedric's ire was sufficiently raised at his sister's blatant lack of consideration. Their own little Sophia had an appearance that many believed to be ghastly, and they loved her in spite of it. But before he could speak, she was turning on her heel and storming out of the room.

He stared after her for a moment before turning back to his mother. The dowager duchess looked very displeased with her daughter's behavior, which Cedric found a relief.

"Forgive your sister, darling," she said after a long moment of silence. "I am sure she means no harm with her words."

Cedric nodded again, remaining quiet. *Let her explain that to her niece, should Sophia ever hear such an outburst,* he thought bitterly.

"I do hope, one day, she comes to understand the gravity of such words," he mumbled, his mood darkening.

The duchess nodded, her face still troubled.

"I hope so, too, darling," she said.

They made small talk for a time, about the weather and the upcoming Season, clearly trying to lighten the mood after Olivia's childish, cruel outburst. Cedric tried to set aside his thoughts about his sister.

He supposed that, because of her young age and her lack of empathy for people who looked a little different, like little Sophia, it was natural for her to behave in such a way. Still, he wondered what kind of effect it might have on his daughter if Olivia ever treated her in such a harsh way.

It also made him wonder what could be wrong with Miss Stewart that would make his sister call her ghastly. He had never heard rumors of a beastly looking woman within the *ton.* But then, he never paid much heed to gossip. So long as the governess had a tolerance for his daughter's affliction, that was all he cared about.

As the meal drew to a close, Cedric realized that he had not discussed the most important current issue with his family before Olivia had stormed off.

"Is everything ready for our move to the country, Mother?" he asked.

The duchess nodded.

"It is, indeed," she said. "I shall go and fetch Olivia and ensure she is ready. She, Sophia, and I will leave today, so we can prepare the staff for your arrival, as well as that of the new governess."

Cedric gave his mother an approving smile

"Very good," he said. "I will leave first thing in the morning, then. I will also order the servants to see that Olivia's and your things are loaded before you depart."

"Wonderful, darling," she said.

He finished eating, then walked over to his mother. He kissed her on the cheek.

"I hope your journey is a safe one," he said.

"May yours tomorrow be safe, as well, dear," she said.

With another smile, Cedric left the room, setting out first to give the staff their orders. He spent the rest of the morning getting all his affairs in order and arranging for the servants to load his things onto the carriage for the following morning. Then, after a brief farewell to his mother, and a rather frosty one from his sister, he headed up to his bedchambers.

He had one final thing to do in London before leaving for their countryseat. And, after seeing his mother and sister off, he went to get ready himself.

Two hours later, his carriage pulled up in front of White's. He saw the familiar figure he sought instantly; the fellow having apparently arrived just before himself. Cedric stepped out of the carriage and approached the man, just as he began looking around, undoubtedly for Cedric.

"Edgar, my friend," Cedric said, holding out his hand.

Edgar Burton, the Viscount Burtondale, grinned at him, taking his hand and shaking it.

"Cedric," he said, "I was unsure whether you would make it."

Cedric rolled his eyes.

"And you yourself have been here a whole, what, two minutes?" he teased.

Edgar shook his head, looking horrified.

"I have been here five whole minutes," he said. "Another two minutes and I would have written you off and gotten drunk without you."

Cedric laughed.

"I have no doubt of that, my friend," he said, wagging his eyebrows.

Edgar narrowed his eyes at his friend, before chuckling.

"You talk bravely now, old fellow," he said, gesturing toward the club, "but we have yet to break out our dealing box."

Cedric winked at his friend.

"My talk shall not change, Ed," he said. "Lead the way to the dealing box. And to your coin purse."

The two men laughed as they entered White's, each promising to clean out each other's pockets. Cedric followed Edgar to his favorite booth at the back of the club, taking the liberty of ordering the first drinks of the evening.

"Is that your resignation to me, before the game has even begun?" Edgar asked.

Cedric snorted.

"Not at all," he said. "It is your consolation prize for whenever you lose."

Edgar laughed enthusiastically.

The drinks arrived shortly thereafter, and the two men toasted to a fun evening of good sport. After their first hearty sips, Cedric looked at his friend.

"How are you finding the Season so far?" he asked.

Edgar sighed, grimacing.

"Have you ever had to chaperone a young woman during those abhorrent seasons?" he asked, rubbing his hair dramatically. "It is very tiresome, indeed. I wonder if my sanity will..."

Cedric glowered at Edgar, until his friend remembered himself.

"Oh, forgive me," he said awkwardly. "Of course, you know how that is. How foolish of me."

Cedric nodded, looking at his friend with sympathy.

"I take it, then, that it has not been going as you hoped?" he asked.

Edgar sighed again.

"Well, I had truly hoped it would go much better," he admitted. "But I still believe Isabel will find a good husband."

Cedric listened patiently. It looked as if Edgar believed anything but that his sister would find a suitable match. But Cedric had an idea.

"You are welcome to bring your sister to the house party I will be hosting at my countryseat," he said. "I would be happy to help you introduce her to some of the men who will be attending."

Edgar smiled at Cedric gratefully.

"You would do that for us?" he asked. "Even though you are already dutifully chaperoning Olivia?"

Cedric shrugged nonchalantly.

"Why not?" he asked. "It would be a pleasure to introduce you and Isabel to some business associates and peers." He snorted again, masking it with a cough. "And I might even introduce you to your future wife, while we are at it."

Edgar pulled away from Cedric, looking at him with wild, wide eyes.

"Get thee back, evil demon," he said, hissing at Cedric. "I would no more marry than I would feed my family to a pack of wolves."

Cedric burst into hysterical laughter.

"I predict that, by the end of the season, you will have changed your mind," he said.

It was Edgar's turn to snicker.

"I will take that bet," he said, reaching for the dealing box nearby. "And speaking of bets, let us begin this very minute."

Cedric motioned for the waiter, ordering a second round of drinks. They set up the game, put up the stakes they wished to gamble, and passed the hours with several rounds of faro, and as many more drinks.

It felt good for Cedric to leave his troubles and worries behind for a while, and it seemed as though Edgar felt the same way. He was, indeed, happy to help his dear friend. And he felt sure that he could.

Chapter Three

"I will miss you dearly, Rosie," Grace said, embracing her niece tightly, tears streaming down her cheeks.

"And I shall miss you, Aunt Grace," Rosalie said, fighting back her own tears. "It will be so strange not to be working under the same roof as you."

Her aunt stroked her cheek fondly.

"I am only a letter away, darling," she said, kissing her niece's forehead. "If you need anything, just write to me. And I promise to visit as often as I can."

Rosalie nodded, knowing that would not be often. As housekeeper of Winsdale Manor, her aunt only occasionally got days off. And the trip to see Rosalie would be a long one, taking up much of those days. Still, she knew her aunt meant what she said, and she loved her all the more for it.

"I do not know what I will do without you and the countess," she said.

Her aunt smiled knowingly at her.

"Do not fret, dear," she said. "This will be a whole new beginning for you."

Rosalie nodded, biting her lip. *That is what I am afraid of,* she thought.

Her aunt read her face and shook her head gently.

"The family will love you, just as the earl and countess have," she said.

Rosalie swallowed hard, her lip trembling.

"It is not the family I fear," she said. "I have already met the dowager duchess, and she was as kind as she could be to me. But what of their servants? What if they are just as cruel to me as Lord and Lady Winsdale's always were?"

As she spoke, she brushed the hideous birthmark on her cheek. The offensive splotch on her cheek had caused her much shame and discomfort. The only people to ever treat her with kindness had been her father, her aunt, and Lord and Lady Winsdale.

Everyone else, including her fellow employees, had treated her like a monster, and most had no trouble calling her such. She was thrilled to have a new job, but she dreaded the prospect of having to relive the initial looks of horror and disgust on the faces of the duke and dowager duchess's servants when she arrived.

Her aunt hugged her again.

"You are beautiful, darling," she said, kissing the horrific dark patch on her cheek. "I think you will find that you worry yourself over nothing."

Rosalie nodded, trying to look brave, but she had never been so uncertain. What if her aunt was wrong? What if the duke and dowager duchess dismissed her because she made the servants uncomfortable?

"Miss Stewart," the butler said, interrupting the two women. "The Livinwood carriage has arrived."

Rosalie's heart leapt into her throat. It was too late to change her mind now. She took a deep breath, kissing both of her aunt's cheeks and putting on a brave smile.

"I love you, Aunt Grace," she said.

Her aunt looked at her with deep affection.

"And I love you, my darling Rosie," she said. "Safe journey to you."

As she followed the butler down the hallway for the very last time, Lady Winsdale stepped into the manor's entryway. Rosalie tried to hide her tears as she looked bravely at the countess.

"Miss Stewart," the countess said, giving Rosalie a warm smile. "I am glad that I did not miss your departure. I wish to give you my personal thanks for everything you have done for my children over the last several years. You were a magnificent governess, and an absolute delight to have in our employ. We wish you the best of luck in your new endeavor."

Rosalie curtseyed politely, fighting back more tears.

"Thank you, your ladyship," she said, "both for your kind words, and for giving me the chance to work for your family. It has been a pleasure."

The countess dipped her head, still smiling. Rosalie thought again about the contrast between the way the countess treated her and the way her servants did. Truly, if it had not been for her aunt and Lady Winsdale, she would have given up her position long ago.

"Let me see you off myself, dear," she said, putting a hand on Rosalie's shoulder.

Rosalie nodded, choking back sobs. She was relieved to no longer be a burden to the family who had saved her from complete poverty, but she knew she would never be as welcome or feel at home anywhere as much as she did at Winsdale Manor.

She looked back at the manor for as long as she could, until it became invisible from the road. Then, she rested her head against the carriage's window, trying to reassure herself that she was wrong about her fate with her new employers.

It was late in the afternoon when Rosalie arrived at the countryseat of the Livinwood's. She was exhausted from the long journey, which had given her time to escape her worry.

However, the moment her feet touched the ground as she exited the coach, her anxiety returned with a vengeance, lodging in the pit of her stomach. Everything depended on how the family, particularly her new student, reacted to her appearance, and she was terrified.

It was that very terror which caused her to cry out when she felt a sudden tug at the bottom of her dress. She jumped back, her heart racing as she looked down at the ground.

As soon as she saw the source of the tugging, however, her heart melted. A sweet little pug had rushed, unseen, up to her and was busy trying to crawl up her dress.

"Oh, you little dear," she murmured, reaching down to pet the excited animal. "Wherever did you come from?"

The dog continued reaching up her dress, smudging it with dirty paw prints, its tongue dangling from its mouth as it painted happily. Rosalie considered stooping down to pick up the animal, but as she was at her new employer's home, she decided against it.

Just then, Rosalie heard a child shouting. She looked back up to see a little girl running toward her, nearly tripping over her own dress as she sped along. The girl's cheeks were flushed, and her gaze was fixed firmly on the dog at Rosalie's feet.

"Princess," the child cried, reaching for the animal, "bad girl! You must never run from me like that. You could be eaten by wild animals."

Rosalie hid a giggle behind her hand. She thought it most likely that the dog had only come running because of the newly arrived carriage, with a new person inside. She said nothing, however, and retracted her hand from the dog's head as the girl picked her up.

The little girl met Rosalie's eyes, her own eyes wide. Rosalie noted with awe that she had one blue eye and one brown eye. She flushed as she waited for the girl to start shrieking about the blotch on her face.

"I am truly sorry," she said, glancing at the squirming dog in her arms. "Princess does not normally do such things." She paused, looking down at the dirt streaks and paw prints on the dress. "Oh dear, she has absolutely ruined your dress. Please, do forgive me."

Rosalie stared for a moment in shock. The child was looking at her with pleading, but not horrified, eyes. She did not seem disgusted by Rosalie's appearance. Rather, she seemed only concerned because Rosalie's dress was dirty. It took her a moment to let her heart settle in her chest, but then, she smiled at the girl.

"It is quite all right," she said, kneeling down so that she was eye level with the child. "You need not worry yourself. I am very fond of dogs, and I think Princess here is most precious."

Relief replaced the mortified expression on the girl's face, and she smiled at Rosalie. But before she could say anything more, someone else came running up to them. Rosalie stood to find herself face to face with a young, flustered looking woman. Her hair was disheveled beneath her bonnet, her cheeks were red, and her eyes flashed with agitation. She wrinkled her nose at Rosalie before turning to the child.

"Sophia," she said, wagging a finger at the girl, "you must never run away from me like that."

Sophia looked at Rosalie again, her eyes wide once more, and she grimaced. Rosalie's stomach twisted into knots at the child's expression. That was the expression she was accustomed to seeing on the faces of others, and the one she had feared seeing on the girl's own. Rosalie looked away just as the young woman grabbed Sophia's hand and marched her back toward the manor. Rosalie stood rooted until they were well out of sight. Then, she made the rest of the short trip up to the front door of the Livinwood country manor.

When she knocked on the large, glossy, oak door, the butler ushered her inside the brightly furnished manor. The drapes, carpets, and chairs were in shades of white, blue, and red, respectively, and gold vases held fresh, exotic-looking flowers that Rosalie could not identify. Their fragrances were as intoxicating as they were new, and Rosalie paused to breathe deeply of them. Already, she felt at ease at the manor, and she was excited to meet the family.

Her bravado only lasted until the duchess met her in one of the winding hallways. The woman's smile was warm, but it made Rosalie once more acutely aware of her discomfort regarding her appearance. She was furious with herself for having forgotten to pull her bonnet down over her face. But it was too late for that concern. She simply curtseyed, trying to keep her voice calm when she spoke.

"Good day, Lady Livinwood," she said with a polite smile. "I hope I am not late."

The duchess laughed softly, reaching out to pat her on the arm.

"Relax, dear," she said. "You are right on time. I trust the trip here went well."

Rosalie nodded.

"Indeed, it did," she said.

Lady Livinwood nodded. Then, she turned behind her and motioned for another young woman to come forward. Rosalie tensed immediately, fighting the urge to flee.

"Miss Stewart, this is Beth, our head housekeeper," the duchess said. "She has been tasked with showing you around and helping you to get settled in. The other servants will bring your belongings in for you, as I am sure you must be weary."

Rosalie nodded as the duchess spoke, not letting on that she had already met Sophia. She did not wish to get the girl in trouble, especially over such an innocent encounter. To that end, she did her best to stand so that the dirty spot on her dress was hidden from the duchess.

When she finished, Rosalie gave the housekeeper a timid smile.

"It is a pleasure to meet you, Beth," she said. "My name is Rosalie Stewart."

Beth beamed at her, taking one of her hands and shaking it gently.

"The pleasure is mine, Rosalie," she said. "And I am happy to show you around."

Rosalie's smile became more genuine as she looked into the housekeeper's round face. She was plump and short, and seemed every bit as warm and kind.

The duchess seemed pleased with their interaction. She dismissed the women, disappearing back down the hall and leaving them to get acquainted.

"I will give you only a brief tour today," Beth said, linking her arm through Rosalie's. "I know you must be exhausted after such a journey."

Rosalie nodded gratefully.

"I am," she said.

As promised, Beth took her quickly and showed her the most immediately important rooms; the drawing room and study, lest she be summoned to either of them, the servant's kitchen, where she would take her meals, the parlor, the servant's entrance, and a few other rooms. It was hard for Rosalie to keep track, but she learned enough to help her find her way around on her own.

"Oh, before I forget," Beth said, pausing their walk. "There are three servants you will likely encounter frequently. They are Irene, Sophia's nursemaid, Barbara, the cook, and, of course, me. But if you need, I can always rendezvous with them for you, rather than you having to run all over the manor trying to find them. That is part of my job, anyway."

Rosalie giggled as Beth mimicked dashing around madly.

"I will remember that," she said. "Thank you, Beth."

Beth nodded, continuing on through the corridors. Rosalie made no mention, even to Beth, of her chance meeting with Sophia the day before, or of the fact that, if she was correct, she had already met Irene. She did not want to remember the look on the young woman's face, especially since she felt so warm and happy that Beth was being kind to her. Instead, she continued to follow Beth along, remaining silent, except for when Beth spoke to her.

"Where did you work before you came here?" Beth asked as they neared the end of their tour.

Rosalie told her about Lord and Lady Winsdale, and Beth smiled sweetly.

"Oh, yes, the Dowager Lady Livinwood thinks very highly of the earl and countess," she said. "Everyone says they are very kind people. I think you will find that His Grace and the dowager are just as amiable and nice. I have worked for them since I was sixteen, and they have always been good to me. Most of the rest of the servants say the same."

Rosalie nodded, but she bit her lip. She wondered if she should mention her insecurities about her birthmark, as Beth acted as though she had not noticed it at all. But she was afraid. If the housekeeper really had not seen it, she could turn on her in an instant.

Beth led her to her bedchambers, seeming to sense her apprehension.

"Is there something else you need?" she asked. "I would be happy to fetch it for you."

Rosalie shook her head, only realizing that she was stroking her blemish when her cheek pressed against her fingertips. She quickly moved her hand, blushing.

"No, you have been wonderful," she said. "Thank you for being so kind."

Beth glanced then at her cheek, and Rosalie braced herself. But Beth just smiled and patted Rosalie on the back.

"You are a very lovely person, Rosalie," she said. "I look forward to being good friends with you."

Rosalie's heart soared. She had never had a true friend before. Not one who was not related to her. Her old bosses were indeed nice, but they were too far above her station to truly be her friends. And Beth was offering her friendship freely and with sincerity.

"I look forward to that, as well, Beth," she said, feeling overwhelmed with joy.

Beth nodded, patting her once more before excusing herself to return to her duties. Rosalie was left to relax and await the arrival of her belongings. She sat by the window, pleased with how well the day had gone so far. Perhaps this would not be such a horrible transition after all. Maybe things would start to be different for her, at last.

Chapter Four

Rosalie awoke early the following morning, surprised at how well she had slept. She supposed she had the long journey to thank for her fatigue, and Beth's kindness the previous evening had helped her to relax easily.

However, as she dressed in the gray dress the dowager duchess had provided for her, her nerves returned. She would soon meet the other servants. Would they be as kind as Beth?

She gave herself a mental shake as she finished pinning up her hair into a tight bun. She wanted to make friends with the servants, of course, but she had another focus that must take precedence.

She needed to make a good impression on the duke and his mother. They were, after all, the ones who could either continue or remove her from employment with them. And she could not let her fear make her so distracted that she failed to satisfy them.

Ready at last, Rosalie made her way to the kitchen of the servant's quarters, which she had seen as Beth had led her to her bedroom. She had her best smile on her face, trying her best to forget all about the birthmark on her cheek. Perhaps if she ignored it, the rest of the servants would, too. But the reaction that she got came as no surprise.

Conversation buzzed when she entered the kitchen. It was the nursemaid, whom Beth had told Rosalie was called Irene, who noticed her first. Rosalie gave her an extra warm smile, glad to see another familiar face. But instead of returning the smile, the young sullen woman frowned. Rosalie winced as the nursemaid turned to the maids sitting directly around her and whispered something inaudible to Rosalie.

When they all turned to stare at her all at once, Rosalie knew immediately what was happening. They all wore various expressions of disgust and then began whispering amongst themselves. Rosalie's fears were being realized, and she felt terribly insecure and vulnerable.

Her aunt had been wrong, as she had suspected. The servants here would be no less forgiving of her birthmark than Lord and Lady Winsdale's had been. She cast her eyes downward and focused on forcing back the tears which threatened to fill her eyes.

The sound of the kitchen door opening made Rosalie freeze. She could not bring herself to look at the person entering, too worried that it would be yet another person who found her as repulsive as the other maids clearly did. But when the person spoke, Rosalie's breath caught.

"May I have your attention, please," Beth said in a loud, commanding voice.

Even though her words were more of a statement than a question, the other servants turned toward her and murmured in the affirmative.

Beth gave Rosalie a quick but warm smile before continuing.

"His Grace will be arriving shortly. We all must be on our best behavior for when we welcome the duke. Is that clear?"

The maids mumbled in agreement, trying their best to appear as innocent as young children. Beth's gaze was unrelenting, however, and they all returned to their meals, quietly, keeping their eyes to their own dishes.

Beth then turned to Rosalie, her face softening.

"Come, Rosalie," she said, sitting at a small table nearest to the kitchen door and motioning for Rosalie to join her. "I would speak with you, if that is all right."

Rosalie nodded, fetching her own portion of breakfast and sitting across from Beth.

"Thank you," Rosalie mouthed, trying not to look at the other servants.

Beth shook her head, looking at Rosalie with kind eyes.

"Think nothing of it," she whispered, leaning in close. "Are you all right?"

Rosalie nodded, giving the housekeeper a wry smile.

"It was to be expected," she said, reflexively touching her face. "Is there something you wish from me?"

Beth nodded, keeping her voice low as she replied.

"The dowager has requested a meeting with you after you have finished breakfast," she said.

Rosalie's heart stopped. Her worst fear was about to be confirmed. The little girl she had encountered upon her arrival would have told the duchess of her hideous appearance, and she would no doubt be eager to dismiss Rosalie from her position. What was left of her appetite dissolved, but she tried to look calm.

"Did she say why?" she asked.

Beth shrugged.

"I cannot say," she said. "Though I would imagine that she wishes you to meet Miss Sophia."

Rosalie nodded, her heart beating wildly in her chest. Was Beth right? Or was she about to be dismissed on her very first day?

She forced herself to spoon a few bites of the plain porridge into her mouth as she collected her thoughts. Then, she excused herself to go and meet with the duchess as requested.

Beth rose with her.

"Would you like me to escort you to her?" she asked.

Rosalie shook her head, despite wishing that Beth would walk with her.

"It is all right," she said. "I shall meet with her on my own." *I shall face my fate as quietly as possible,* she added silently.

Beth nodded.

"Very well," she said. "She will be waiting for you in the drawing room. And please, do not hesitate to come and fetch me if you need anything."

Rosalie nodded.

"Thank you," she said.

Carefully avoiding the glaring eyes of the rest of the servants, Rosalie made her way out of the servant's kitchen and into the main hallways of the manor. She focused on slowing her breathing as she approached the drawing room.

Whatever awaited her when she entered the room, she resolved to face it with all the strength she could muster. She took a deep breath and pushed through the half-closed door, curtseying as soon as she was in the room.

"You asked to see me, my lady?" she asked.

The dowager duchess looked up and smiled at her, motioning her over to where she sat. Rosalie noticed then that beside her was the little girl from the day before, as well as the little dog that had greeted her. Before Lady Livinwood had even introduced them, Rosalie confirmed her suspicions that the blue-and-brown eyed girl was, indeed, her tutoring charge. She held her breath as the child looked up from Princess and met her eyes. She had put the grimace she last saw on the girl's face out of her mind until that very moment. But now that Sophia was looking at her again, she waited to see it once more.

"Miss Stewart, this is our dear little Sophia, and her beloved Princess," she said, smiling fondly at the young girl.

Rosalie immediately curtseyed to the child, her heart pounding too loudly for her to speak. Fortunately, the duchess was not waiting for her to do so. As soon as she righted herself, the older woman beckoned her to sit down between her and the girl.

"Please, Miss Stewart, join us for a moment," she said.

Rosalie nodded, fighting the urge to chew on her lip. It would not do to give herself a bloody cut on her mouth on her very first day of employment. Certainly not one caused by her own doing. Gently, she sat between the duchess and Sophia, waiting for the girl's reaction.

"Sophia, dear, Miss Stewart is your new governess," the duchess said.

Rosalie took a deep breath at the girl. The dog, clearly remembering her, as well, began squirming excitedly in the child's lap. Rosalie had to force herself to keep her hand in her lap and resist the urge to pet the dog. She did not know if the girl had told the duchess about their encounter the previous day, and she did not want to be the one to mention it if she had not.

After what seemed like ages, the little girl smiled sweetly at Rosalie.

"I am pleased to meet you, Miss Stewart," she said, pointing to the dog. "And this is Princess."

Rosalie felt great warmth in her chest as the girl smiled. It was genuine and kind, without a trace of horror or distaste. Rosalie gave her a nod, returning her smile.

"Likewise, Miss Sophia," she said. "And I am pleased to meet Princess, too."

Sophia beamed at Rosalie at the mention of her dog

"You can pet her, if you like," she said, winking at Rosalie. "I think she likes you."

Rosalie bit her lip to keep from giggling as she extended her hand to the animal. Princess was thrilled, immediately taking the opportunity to crawl into Rosalie's lap.

"Sophia," the duchess said in a gently admonishing tone, "Miss Stewart may not appreciate Princess pawing her to death."

Rosalie looked at her employer and smiled.

"I love dogs," she said. "If it does not bother you, I am quite fine with Princess sitting with me."

Lady Livinwood's face relaxed, and she, too, smiled.

"I do not mind at all," she said, nodding at Rosalie with kind approval. "Though, I hope that dear Sophia can teach Princess not to climb on everyone in such a manner."

Sophia giggled, sensing nothing but love in her grandmother's voice.

"Of course, I will, Grandmother," she said. "Maybe Miss Stewart can help me teach her?"

The duchess looked at Sophia patiently.

"Darling, I am sure Miss Stewart will be far too busy with your lessons," she said. "And afterward, I imagine she will be tired. Do not put too much on your new governess now, Sophia."

Rosalie petted the dog, murmuring a soft command in her ear. Instantly, the dog laid down, getting perfectly still and calm in her lap.

Sophia gasped.

"How did you do that?" she asked.

Rosalie shrugged bashfully, glancing at the duchess's impressed expression.

"I truly do love dogs," she said. "I used to have one as a pet myself. I taught him a few things."

Sophia's eyes lit up.

"What was his name?" she asked.

Rosalie smiled, thinking fondly of her dog. He had died when she was young, but she still found his memory comforting to her.

"Rascal," she said. "Because when he was a puppy, he used to chew all of my father's shoes. Until that was, I worked with him, and I started making him toys of his own to chew."

The duchess gasped, and Sophia clapped her hands.

"Could you help me with Princess?" she asked.

Rosalie remembered what her grandmother had just said.

"Let us focus on your lessons," she said. "But perhaps, on days when you finish early, I can show you a few things that might help train her."

Lady Livinwood nodded with approval once more. Sophia squealed with delight, jumping up to hug her grandmother.

The moment was interrupted by the entrance of the butler.

"My lady," he said, bowing, "His Grace has just arrived.

The duchess rose, and Rosalie followed suit, her heart lodging in her throat.

"Come, dear," she said to Sophia. "We must prepare to greet your father. Miss Stewart, if you would come with us, I will show you where to stand."

Rosalie followed behind silently, her pulse racing. She was about to meet the duke of the family. Would he be as warm and friendly as his mother and daughter were? Or would he be cold and cruel, like Irene and the servants?

Chapter Five

Cedric sighed with relief as the carriage pulled into the driveway of his countryseat. It was almost noon, and he knew that his mother and sister, who had come separately ahead of him with little Sophia to meet the new governess, would likely be preparing for lunch soon. He hoped that was the case, at least, as the journey had left him weary and hungry.

However, he had to admit it was a worthwhile trip. He was genuinely happy to be away from London for a while. In his twelve years as duke, he had rarely taken any kind of vacation.

He had spent time overseas for business, but it had been ages since he'd retired to his country home and oversaw his business matters from there. It would be lovely to spend some time in the country, in the peace and quiet and fresh air.

When he stepped from the carriage, he was met by liveried footmen who greeted him formally and then began fetching his things from the coach.

The butler was waiting at the door with a warm smile, bowing as he welcomed his master. Inside, lining the hallway, were all the household servants, standing in a straight line. He smiled at them, each man and woman in his employ giving him bows and curtseys, respectively, as he made his way along the line.

At the end of the line was his mother, who greeted him with kisses on the cheek and relief for his safe trip. Beside his mother stood his dear Sophia, who was beaming up at him. He grinned, preparing to scoop her up into his arms. But just then, he noticed she was holding the hand of a woman wearing a plain gray dress. At once he recognized the dress as the governess's uniform.

He looked at the woman, preparing to introduce himself, but he noticed that though she had curtseyed to him, just as the other servants had, she would not look directly at him. Not only that, but she had a big bonnet pulled tightly over her face.

Perplexed, Cedric motioned for the butler to dismiss the rest of the servants. The governess fortunately stayed, albeit appearing uncomfortable, until the rest of the staff had filed out of the hallway and returned to their duties.

With everyone else gone, Cedric noticed that someone was missing.

"Where is Olivia?" he asked with a frown, briefly turning from the new governess to look at his mother.

The dowager duchess sighed.

"Your sister complained of a megrim," she said. "She has stayed in her bedchambers to rest."

Cedric nodded.

"I hope she feels better soon," he said.

His mother smiled, glancing at the new governess, returning Cedric's attention to her, as well.

"Darling, this is Rosalie Stewart," she said, giving the woman a warm smile. "She will be our new governess, as I am sure you have surmised."

Cedric turned to her with a smile. This time, she was looking at him, and he saw that her eyes were the most mesmerizing shade of jade green he had ever seen. Though he still could not see most of her face, he was drawn to her eyes. She held his gaze, but she looked terribly uncomfortable.

He considered requesting that she loosen her bonnet during the introductions, but something in her eyes made him feel as though she was pleading with him not to do so. But what?

A tug on his jacket pulled him from his daze. He shook his head and looked down into his daughter's smiling face. Her eyes sparkled, which eased his mind a little. Sophia had clearly met the new governess before him, and she did not look afraid or sad. He smiled back at her, bending down to kiss her on top of her head.

"What is it, darling?" he asked.

Sophia took one of his hands in her small ones and began swinging it gently.

"Papa, when will you be taking me to the stables?" she asked. "You know how I love horses, and I wish to see one up close."

Cedric laughed. It was not the first time his daughter had asked that question, but it was the first time she had done so in such a direct fashion.

"Sophia, dear, you are a bit small yet," he said. "You will need to wait until you are older before visiting the horses."

Sophia's smile dissolved, and she set her jaw. In that moment, she looked much like her mother, and Cedric had to bite back another chuckle.

"I am eight years old, Papa," she reminded him. "I am hardly a little child anymore. Please, oh please, will you take me to the stables? I will stay right with you, and I will not approach any horse without you beside me. Please?"

Cedric thought it over for a minute. She was, indeed, still very small. But maybe he could consider taking her when the horses were all locked in their stalls. It was something he needed to consider further, so he gave her an indulgent smile.

"I will think about it," he said. "For now, however, you must be a good girl and go with Miss Stewart to the schoolroom."

Sophia thought over her father's words, glancing at the governess. Then, she looked back up at him and smiled once more.

"All right, Papa," she said. "But I shall not forget that you said you would think about it."

Cedric laughed again.

"I have no doubt, darling," he said, kissing her once more. "Now, run along, and be good for Miss Stewart."

Sophia nodded. She took the governess's hand and began to lead her in the direction of the schoolroom. Cedric looked at the young woman as she turned away, and he noted that she looked incredibly relieved to be dismissed.

It was clear she was very uncomfortable there, but he could not understand why. He said nothing further, however. He simply gestured for the woman to take Sophia upstairs. Then, he turned and offered his arm to his mother.

"Shall we take tea?" he asked.

The duchess put her arm in his and gestured with her hand.

"Lead the way, dear," she said.

The servants were just arriving with the trays of tea and treats when they entered the drawing room. As they helped themselves, Cedric thought about the new governess.

He had been expecting a woman who looked akin to a monster. And yet, all he had seen were beautiful jade green eyes, which he still could not get out of his mind, and lovely skin. What of it he could see, at least.

At last, the mystery was too much for him to bear. He set aside his teacup and pastries and looked at his mother.

"I do not understand something," he said. "I met Miss Stewart myself, only moments ago. And yet, I saw nothing that would classify her as ghastly, as Olivia says everyone calls her."

The duchess paused for a moment, seeming to think carefully before she spoke. She took a long sip of tea, resting it gently in her lap when she finished.

"She uses her bonnet to cover up most of her face," she said. "I trust you noticed that, as well."

Cedric shrugged. He had, and he had wanted to ask her to remove it, at least for the sake of proper introductions. But the fear in her eyes had made him reconsider. Now, he wished he had insisted.

"I could see as much," he said. "But should she not have pulled it back upon meeting us? Is she so fearful of judgment and ridicule that she will not even remove it for her employers?"

To his surprise, the duchess nodded, her eyes sad.

"Indeed, she is," she said quietly. "The poor girl is very kind and smart, and Lady Winsdale assures me she is a wonderful governess. But she is very insecure about her appearance."

Cedric could not help but laugh. His mother gave him a sharp look, but he held up his hands in defense.

"I do not laugh at her, Mother," he said. "But there are women all over London alone who look more like men, or dogs, than women. A woman as young as Miss Stewart, who does not appear to be those women, should have nothing to fear. Least of all from us."

His mother nodded, her own mouth twitching for a moment.

"You are wicked, dear," she said. "But remember that those women cannot help their beastly appearance, either. We must never laugh at the misfortune of such people. There, but for the grace of God, go we, after all."

Cedric blushed. He knew his mother had a point. He supposed it was his curiosity driving him mad. Instead of making anymore crude remarks, he decided to get right to the point of the matter.

"What is it about her face that is flawed?" he asked.

The duchess once more paused, this time putting a treat she was about to bite back on the plate.

"It is not my place to tell you that, darling," she said. "You can speak with her yourself if you wish. But I have no doubt you will see for yourself soon enough."

Cedric nodded thoughtfully. He supposed his mother was right. It was rude to gossip about someone, especially someone he did not know. But now his curiosity was genuinely piqued.

Was she scarred from some accident? Was it possible she had a similar condition with her eyes as Sophia? He wanted to press on and ask questions, but deep down, he knew it was not proper.

"Of course, Mother," he said. "I trust your judgment. If she was pleasant and skilled enough for you to hire her, then she is good enough for Sophia and me."

The duchess smiled knowingly.

"You shall not regret it, darling," she said. "And I trust that you will be far more accepting and understanding than your sister has been thus far."

Cedric looked at his mother as though she had just pointed out a sea creature swimming outside the window.

"Of course, I will, Mother," he said. "I am well aware of how judgmental others can be, even of people with good, kind souls. I also know how harsh and hurtful it can be to those who are being judged. I have spent the last eight years trying to shelter Sophia from the cruelty of the outside world. I hope that one day, I am successful with that."

His mother gave him a proud, affectionate look.

"I think you have done a marvelous job, dear," she said. "But you will not be around to protect her forever. But I believe she now has a kind, compassionate governess, one who understands her affliction, and who can teach her how to be proud of who she is."

Cedric tilted his head.

"But you said that Miss Stewart is very self-conscious," he said.

His mother nodded, raising an eyebrow.

"I never said that our little Sophia would not be teaching her, as well," she said.

With a quick kiss on his cheek, she excused herself to give the evening's dinner menu to the cook. Cedric was left wondering what his mother meant. There was one thing he knew for sure: If he wanted answers, he needed to see the governess's face himself. What about it could possibly be so bad?

Chapter Six

"Let us go," Sophia said, both of her eyes sparkling with their own unique excitement.

Rosalie smiled at her again, letting the child lead her up the stairs. She tried to keep her face calm and pleasant, despite the turmoil she felt. But her encounter with the duke had rattled her, and she was more than relieved to be away from his handsome, but intimidating, smile.

"You seem very eager for your lessons," she said.

Sophia shrugged.

"I enjoy my lessons sometimes," she said. "But mostly, I wish to get them finished for the day, so I can go play."

Rosalie giggled.

"Fair enough," she said. "Well, I shall try to make them go by as fast as possible."

Sophia nodded happily as they turned a corner.

"Guess what, Miss Stewart?" the little girl asked.

"What, Sophia?" she asked, sharing the child's infectious joy.

"I have taught Princess a new trick," she said, her eyes brighter than before.

Rosalie gasped with genuine surprise.

"Did you now?" she asked. "What trick is that?"

"I taught her to roll over," she said, unable to contain her excitement as she pulled away from Rosalie to jump up and down and clap her hands.

Rosalie's mouth fell open. She knew that small dogs were fairly easy to train. But for a girl so young to do it so easily was astonishing to her.

"That is wonderful, Sophia," she said. "Tell me how you did it."

The little girl was happy to oblige.

"Well, I sneaked some beef from dinner in my dress pocket a couple of nights in a row," she said, dropping her voice conspiratorially. "And after Irene tucked me into bed, I got up and practiced with Princess. And each time she did it, I would give her a little piece of beef. Now, she can do it every time I tell her to."

Rosalie giggled. She loved the child's spirit already. She reminded her of herself when she was young.

"That is marvelous, dear," she said, grinning. "You are very loving and skilled with Princess."

Sophia nodded proudly.

"Having Princess is so much fun," she said. Then, she lowered her voice once more. "Please do not tell Papa that I sneak meat from my meals."

Rosalie's heart swelled. The child was already trusting her with a big secret, which filled her with even more affection for the young girl.

"I promise to not tell a soul, darling," she whispered back, winking at the girl.

Rosalie was so enraptured by the young girl's enthusiasm and smiles that she did not see a figure approaching from further down the hallway. In fact, she would have bumped into the prim and proper young lady, had Sophia not done so first, making her stop in her tracks. Rosalie looked at the woman's face, which was twisted with disdain and disgust. Rosalie swallowed hard, looking away and praying the woman would continue on her way.

"Miss Stewart," Sophia said, running up to embrace the woman. "This is my Aunt Olivia.

Rosalie flushed, dipping immediately into a curtsey. She should have known this was the duke's sister. She was present when His Grace mentioned her, after all. She hoped she would recover from her ignorance and make a good impression on Lady Olivia.

"Good day, my lady," Rosalie said, struggling to meet her eyes once more. "My name is—"

"I know precisely who you are," Olivia snapped. "And I do not have time for such introductions."

Rosalie gaped as the young woman pushed past her, without a single word to her niece, who looked confused. Rosalie was shocked, as well, and she scrambled to gather her thoughts to salvage the mood for the little girl. However, it was the little girl who spoke first.

"Miss Stewart," she said, taking Rosalie's hand again and beaming up at her. "Do not worry about Aunt Olivia. She is always in a bad mood. She's really very nice once you get to know her."

Rosalie nodded, trying to hide her dubious expression from the child. The girl was innocent, and she could not understand the way her aunt had looked at the governess. But Rosalie knew that look well, and she suspected the rude outburst was more than just a bad mood.

She had seen that same look too many times in her life to believe the woman was not horrified by her. What puzzled Rosalie, though, was that she had not looked shocked. Though Olivia was clearly disgusted, she did not seem surprised by Rosalie's deformity.

Realizing that Sophia was looking up at her expectantly, Rosalie forced herself to dismiss the thoughts. There was no point in overthinking the encounter. Perhaps it was just as Sophia said, her aunt was simply in a bad mood. It was not for Rosalie to judge or assume, as she did not know the young woman.

"Let us get to your lessons, dear," she said, trying to give the child a bright smile.

Sophia grinned and nodded.

"The schoolroom is just down there," she said, pointing.

Rosalie followed the girl down the hall and into the open door of the schoolroom. Rosalie was awestricken as she looked around at the learning materials and supplies. Everything appeared to be brand-new and of the most up-to-date quality. Even the slate was clean and free of scratches, as though it had just been placed on the wall that very morning. Rosalie had never seen anything quite like it, and she found herself growing excited to begin Sophia's lessons.

"Well," she said, turning back to Sophia, who had already climbed into her seat and was waiting on further instructions. "I suppose I should first know where you left off with your last governess. It would be senseless to teach you something you already know."

To Rosalie's surprise, the girl looked down at her desk, seeming suddenly uncomfortable.

"She did not teach me much," she said, so softly that Rosalie had to strain to hear her. "She was not here long enough, really."

Rosalie frowned. She wondered what would make someone wish to leave such a sweet child. Clearly, Sophia was very polite, and she seemed excited about her lessons. Why should anyone walk away from such a delightful task? Had she been too strict and got herself dismissed?

She considered asking the girl, but it was clear she was unhappy at the mere thought. Rosalie certainly did not wish to jeopardize her own job by upsetting Sophia. Besides, she knew that look on the child's face; she saw it on her own more often than she cared to admit. She could never put the girl through anything to make that expression worsen.

"Well, I will be here for a very long time, if you will have me," she said.

Sophia instantly brightened, which made Rosalie feel the now familiar warmth in her heart when someone looked at her.

"Really?" she asked, hopefully.

Rosalie giggled and nodded.

"I promise, darling," she said.

Sophia leapt from her seat and clapped her hands.

"I promise to be a good girl and to finish all the lessons you assign men," she said. "And I am really smart. Papa and Grandmother say so."

Rosalie laughed again.

"I can see that already," she said. "Tell me, which subjects do you like best?"

Sophia's special, beautiful eyes lit up. She thought for a moment, then smiled at Rosalie.

"Well, I like grammar a little," she said. "It feels good when adults tell me how grownup I sound. And I love reading. I think reading is my favorite school subject."

Rosalie nodded in agreement.

"I love to read, too," she said. "What do you like besides school subjects?"

Sophia hopped over to the window, pointing outside.

"I love nature," she said proudly. "And I love painting. But I especially love painting out in nature."

Rosalie's heart squeezed. She thought of the love of sketching she once had, which she missed dearly. Could it be that she was tutoring a child who not only was not terrified of her appearance, but also shared some of her same interests?

"Nature and art go hand in hand, I think," Rosalie said, grinning at the girl. "It sounds as if you and I are going to get along nicely."

She held her breath. She had made a mistake intentionally when speaking. It was her first test for young Sophia.

To her surprise, the child caught it instantly.

"It is supposed to be you and I, Miss Stewart," she corrected.

Rosalie clapped her hands.

"Very good, Sophia," she said. "I knew you were smart. I am very impressed."

The girl beamed proudly.

"You can't fool me, Miss Stewart," she said, winking.

Rosalie giggled.

"And so, I cannot," she said. "Now, tell me which subjects you like the least."

Sophia's eyes widened, and she raised her eyebrow.

"If I tell you, does that mean that we do not have to do them?" she asked.

Rosalie laughed.

"No, darling," she said. "We must do them all. But it will help me to know which ones you are not as fond of before we begin our lessons."

Sophia's face fell again.

"That is too bad," she said. "I really do not like numbers. And I hate learning about decorum. It is nice to impress the grownups and all, but I would really rather be outside playing than learning how *not* to play outside."

Rosalie's frown almost turned into a laugh at the child's words, and she had to bite her lip. She studied the forlorn girl, and an idea occurred to her.

"Can we make a deal?" she asked, winking at Sophia.

At this, Sophia perked up once more, and shrugged.

"What kind of deal?" she asked, intrigued.

Rosalie knelt in front of her, grinning.

"For every lesson on numbers and decorum you complete, I shall reward you with spending some time outside."

Sophia gasped, covering her mouth, but not in time to keep a delighted shriek from escaping.

"Do you mean it?" she asked. "Could we really do that without getting into trouble?"

Rosalie nodded. She felt sure she could talk the duke and duchess into allowing such adventures, though she doubted they would be objective, anyway. They were good people, and they clearly loved Sophia. It was hardly unusual for governesses to take education out into nature, and she was sure they would be agreeable.

"I promise," she said. "Perhaps that will help those lessons not seem so bad."

Sophia did not need time to think. She beamed up at Rosalie, her lovely eyes sparkling once more.

"We have a deal, Miss Stewart," she said.

Chapter Seven

Olivia stood watching the new governess and her niece as they stood in the hallway just down from the schoolroom. She could not hear what the two were saying, but she watched intently. With any luck, she could find some indication that Sophia did not like the woman.

Then, she could report back to her mother and get Rosalie Stewart dismissed. But no such thing happened. Instead, Sophia tugged on the woman's hand and pulled her inside the schoolroom.

When the pair at last disappeared inside the room, Olivia slipped from her hiding place, her temper flaring. Getting Miss Stewart dismissed was clearly out of the question for the time being. But she wasn't just angry with the woman.

She would not even have to be trying to figure out how to get rid of her if her mother had not hired her in the first place. What in the world had her mother been thinking?

Olivia descended the stairs slowly, but with obvious discontent. She could not believe that her mother had not considered their family when choosing *that* woman as governess. The Livinwood's had a good name to uphold. For generations their family had been reputable, honorable, and respectable. Not a single blemish had cast a shadow on her family in the entire history of their dukedom. *Certainly, not one so large as that on the hideous governess's face,* she thought, with huge disdain.

No matter how she tried to figure it out, she could not imagine what could cause her mother to risk their good name by employing that ugly young woman. Everyone in the *ton* knew of her ghastly appearance, and no one approved. If word got around that her family had taken pity on such a hideous monster, it could well be the scandal that ruined their name. But, more importantly to Olivia, it could ruin her chances of finding a good match that Season.

Olivia sighed as she reached the first floor of the manor. Did no one else care about her future? She was determined to find a gentleman with vast wealth and a prestigious title.

But with such a beast living inside the walls of her family home, the chances of such a feat grew dramatically slim. She knew that if she questioned her mother's sanity for making such a decision, the rest of the *ton* would begin to do so, as well.

At last, she dragged herself to the dining room. She had skipped breakfast, but from the looks of it, lunch was just being served. Her mother and brother sat in the dining room, talking amongst themselves. When the duchess saw her, her brow furrowed with concern.

"Olivia, darling," she said. "How are you feeling?"

Olivia smiled brightly, happy that her mother had been fooled. She had, of course, not been ill. She had feigned a megrim just because she wanted to sleep in that morning, rather than rise early to greet her brother when he arrived. She thought it foolish that they had traveled to the country separately to begin with. Why should she drag herself out of bed to greet her own brother?

"I am feeling much better," she said. "Rather hungry, in fact."

Her mother beamed at her, gesturing for her to take her seat.

"I am glad to hear it, darling," she said. "I was worried sick about you."

Cedric left his seat to come to kiss his sister's cheek, which Olivia endured with reluctance.

"As was I, Sister," he said. "It is good to see you well again."

Olivia blushed, hardly feeling guilty about her lie. It was, after all, their fault that the hideous beast upstairs now worked for them. As far as she was concerned, her lie was fair revenge for slighting her with such a decision. But she feigned gratitude and humility as she batted her eyelashes at them.

"I suppose I just needed a little bit more sleep this morning," she said, telling part of the truth. "I hope both of you are well this afternoon."

Her brother spoke first, giving her a wide grin.

"I trust you have not forgotten about our house party," he said.

Olivia gasped softly. She had, in fact, forgotten about it, with her stewing thoughts about the damnable governess. She kept her smile, however, and looked at her mother with enthusiasm.

"I am sure it will be a lovely affair," she said. But her earlier fears of losing out on a good match because of Miss Stewart battled to return to her mind. Perhaps, though, she would stand a better chance of getting the attention of a suitable man at her own family's party. Surely, men would not dismiss her so readily in her own home.

All she would need, for the time being, was to capture the affections of one wealthy man, before he learned about the hideous governess. Maybe then, she could keep the woman from ruining her life.

Cedric smirked at her.

"Your recovery means that you will not miss the chance to find a suitor," he said, echoing her thoughts.

Olivia looked at him smugly.

"Are you jesting, Brother?" she said, pausing to take a bite of the food before her. "I would not miss a party for the world. Especially not our own."

Both her brother and mother nodded.

"We are expecting the finest families in London tomorrow night," the duchess said, winking at her daughter. "Including the finest bachelors."

Olivia brightened despite herself.

"Can we go dress shopping before then?" she asked.

The duchess shook her head, but her expression was mysterious.

"We shall not get new dresses ready in time for tomorrow," she said. "However, I ordered several new outfits before we left London, and they have just arrived. The maid is putting yours in your wardrobe as we speak, so you can look at them when you are ready."

Olivia clapped her hands joyfully.

"Oh, thank you, Mother," she said, turning to Cedric. "And thank you for providing the means, Brother."

Cedric shrugged.

"It was well worth it to see you so happy, Sister," he said. "And I am glad you are now well enough to enjoy it."

Olivia's smile widened, her unhappiness about the new governess temporarily forgotten. With a party to look forward to and new dresses for her to try on when the meal ended, how could she be anything but thrilled?

"I am especially excited for the party now," she said, taking a hearty bite of her food.

Cedric smiled at her.

"It will be lovely," he said. "I even invited some of my personal friends before leaving town. Edgar, my oldest friend, and his sister, have assured me they will be in attendance."

Olivia nearly choked on her food. She cleared her throat, her face flushing. She cared nothing for the gentleman's sister. She could not even recall whether she had ever met the woman. But the viscount himself had her full attention.

"Lord Burtondale?" she asked, failing to sound as casual as she hoped.

"The very same," her brother agreed. "Why?"

Olivia shook her head, her heart racing. She'd had a crush on the Viscount Burtondale for some time, but it had been ages since she had seen him. She thought quickly, trying to find a way to ask about him without seeming too conspicuous. She was not ready to reveal her feelings about the viscount to her family, but her curiosity was burning.

"I have not heard you speak of him in some time," she said, casually stirring her food with her fork. "I trust he is well."

Cedric gave her a curious look, but he nodded.

"He is," he said. "He has agreed to chaperone Miss Burton this Season, to help her find a match."

Olivia pretended to be nonchalantly satisfied with her brother's answer, but her mind was moving in time with her pounding heart.

"Will his wife be joining him at the party?" she asked.

Cedric laughed, startling her. She looked up at her brother with raised eyebrows, waiting for him to explain himself.

"Oh, Sister," he said. "Edgar is not married. I suspect he would rather stick hot pokers in his eyes than find himself a bride."

Olivia giggled despite herself, and she was glad of it; she could not have Cedric suspecting that she had an interest in the viscount. She did not care if it upset him, but she was not prepared to discuss it with him. And she had learned what she wished to know: The man she loved was still a bachelor. Even if he was determined *not* to get married, she still had a chance to change his mind.

"Surely, marriage cannot not be so painful," she said, laughing.

Cedric shrugged, shaking his head.

"If you asked him, I am certain he would disagree," he said.

Olivia nodded, returning to her meal. She was no longer hungry, however. Now she knew the viscount would be attending the party, she had one sole focus. She would do her best to work on gaining his affections during the house party, and she would not let him out of her sight for the entire Season. Nothing would stop her from trying to win Lord Burtondale's heart. Especially not some hideous governess.

Chapter Eight

Cedric sat back, watching his sister with dutiful affection as she talked excitedly with their mother. He could not help noticing she was in a rather good mood.

Clearly, whatever illness had plagued her earlier that morning had long passed, and he was grateful. He loved his sister, and he wanted nothing more for her than for her to be happy and well.

He also wanted to ensure she married well. It was, after all, his responsibility to see to that, since their father was dead, and it was one he took seriously. More seriously, perhaps, than he did the entire duchy. And he could not help reminding himself that Olivia was now in her second Season without a husband. He knew he must do everything he could to ensure she did not have a third.

"Oh, my darlings," the dowager gushed loudly enough to pull Cedric from his thoughts, "I simply cannot wait for our house party."

Cedric smiled warmly. His mother's happiness was important to him too. And while he did not care much for hosting parties, it was clear that doing so brought his mother great joy.

"I am certain it will be a memorable event, Mother," he said.

The duchess nodded, beaming.

"Indeed," she said. "I have hired the finest orchestra in London, and there will be tables filled with delightfully novel refreshments."

Olivia clapped her hands, clearly as pleased as her mother.

"I do hope that some prestigious gentlemen will attend," she said dreamily.

Their mother nodded matter-of-factly.

"There will be many prominent bachelors, darling," she said, turning to Cedric and raising her eyebrows. "And unwed misses, as well."

Cedric pretended to not have noticed his mother's wink as he became suddenly enthralled with the meal before him. He well knew that the duchess was hinting for him to begin seeking a new wife, but he had no interest in doing so. After Bridget died, he had promised himself to never remarry.

He had not loved her in any romantic way, but she had been a dutiful wife and, he believed, taught him everything there was to know about being married. He was happy to remain a widower for the rest of his days.

Yet as he put forkful after forkful of food in his mouth, his mind continued to wander. When it settled on the memory of a certain pair of jade-green eyes, he sighed softly. Those eyes had, indeed, been enthralling, even though he had not gotten a clear look at her entire face. Something in him knew, just from her eyes, that the rest of her must be lovely, as well.

It took great effort to not choke on his meal as he realized he was thinking of the new governess in a very inappropriate fashion. Beautiful eyes or not, she was still in his employ. Even thinking privately about an employee in a romantic way was as dangerous as it was scandalous. He had no idea what could have made him entertain such ideas, but he knew he must cease immediately.

Before he could further scold himself, the butler entered the room, bowing to Cedric.

"Pardon, me, your lordship," he said, "Mr. James has arrived, and he wishes to speak with you. He says it is urgent."

Cedric rose quickly. It was rare that the estate manager made unexpected calls.

"Thank you, Johns," Cedric said. Then, he excused himself from his mother and sister and followed the butler to the entryway, where the businessman waited. After a brief greeting, Cedric led Mr. James to his study. After pouring them each a drink, Cedric sat across from the estate manager at his desk.

"I was not expecting to meet with you until the end of the month," he said. "How can I help you, Mr. James?"

The man wore a sheepish expression as he pulled out some sheets from the stack of papers he was holding and handed them to Cedric.

"I came to see if I could not help *you*, Your Grace," he said. "Or, at the very least, alert you to a rather large problem, before it is too late."

Cedric frowned. He pushed aside his drink and took the pages. He looked through the names and figures, chewing on his lip.

"This is from the rent ledger," he said, confused. "Everything appears to be in order. I do not understand."

Mr. James pointed gently to the second paper Cedric was holding.

"The page you are reading shows the rent that has been paid," he said. "The second one shows the people who have not yet had their rent collected, and how much they owe."

Cedric turned to the second page, but he looked back up at Mr. James.

"Unpaid rent?" he asked. The words hardly made sense. In his years as duke, and as far as he could remember when his father before him reigned over the duchy, there had never been any trouble with tenants paying rent. Cedric read the paper carefully, noting that some of the payments appeared to be more than a month behind.

"I found it very strange too, Your Grace," Mr. James said, nervously sipping his drink. "Typically, any delinquent accounts that your tenants incur are paid within days of the due date. But as you can see there, that has not been the case with some of them for quite some time."

Cedric bit his lip as he tried to make sense of the figures before him. Some of the names he recognized, but others were fairly new, and he had yet to commit their faces to his memory.

"Could it be that some of the families are struggling with their crops or their livestock this year?" he asked. "Have any of the tenants given any reasons as to why they have not paid?

Mr. James shook his head slowly.

"No one has given any reasons, Your Grace," he said. "And I considered the possibility of hardships when the payments were merely considered late. However, after further inspection of the ledgers, I feel there is something more happening."

Cedric looked over the sheet again. Almost half the names on the list were, as Mr. James had said, more than a month behind. The most delinquent, one Mr. Brown, was three months behind, which qualified the family for eviction. But Cedric had never even considered evicting anyone. Nor had his father. What was happening?

"Surely, there is a mistake," he murmured. "How can this be? This is too unusual to be correct. Or there is something very serious happening."

Mr. James nodded eagerly.

"I believe I have a theory," he said. "Though I cannot say for sure."

Cedric handed back the papers to the man, rubbing his forehead.

"Speak on, Mr. James," he said. "I wish to understand, so that we may begin to find a solution as soon as possible."

Mr. James cleared his throat, showing him another paper. The page made no sense to him, but it did make mention of the same Mr. Brown several times. Cedric looked up at him expectantly.

"As you saw, Mr. Brown's account is the one that is the furthest behind on payments," he said. "And on the page you are holding are estimates on his profits from his family's farm. I was able to determine that he has also had a bountiful harvest, which he has been actively selling at stands in the market district. It seems to me that, for some reason, Mr. Brown simply decided to stop paying his rent. And I believe that he is influencing other farmers to do the same."

Cedric blinked, confused.

"But why would he do such a thing?" he asked. "Does he not realize that I will evict him if I absolutely must? Does he not care?"

Mr. James shrugged weakly.

"It is only a theory, Your Grace," he said. "I have no further answers. But it makes logical sense. Not only has the number of non-paying tenants increased, but it seems to be increasing each month. At this rate, the financial impact to your family will be substantial by the end of the year."

Cedric chewed his lip. He tried to recall if his father had ever said anything, for good or ill, about Mr. Brown. He knew the man, but he had only spoken to him personally a few times.

The man had never given him any reason to believe he would willingly default in such a way, and certainly none to suggest he might encourage other farmers to stop paying too. In fact, as far as Cedric he could recall, the man had always been very polite and respectful, and until recently, had tried to ensure he made his rent payments early.

None of it made any sense, and it put Cedric on edge. For all the lessons his father had given him about running the duchy, he had never taught him how to handle such a situation. He supposed the only way to get answers was to go to the tenants themselves. Starting with one in particular.

"Mr. James, thank you for bringing this to my attention," he said, reaching out to shake the man's hand once more. "Forgive me for drawing this meeting to such an abrupt close, but I must pay a visit to Mr. Brown."

Mr. James stood as he shook Cedric's hand, but his expression was dubious.

"Is that wise, Your Grace?" he asked. "I do not wish to make any accusations until we have more information."

Cedric gave him an understanding look.

"I plan only to do exactly that," he said. "I will make no accusations until I have spoken with him and see what he says. And then, you and I will meet again soon and discuss what I learn, and what we should do next."

Mr. James nodded, seeming relieved and satisfied with Cedric's answer.

"Very good," he said, bowing to Cedric. "I will await word from you before I proceed further."

Cedric nodded, gesturing for the butler to see the man out. Then, he headed to the stables, determined to get answers straightaway.

"Lad," he said, beckoning the stable boy to him. "I need a strong horse saddled at once."

Chapter Nine

Rosalie had to struggle to keep her face straight as Sophia recited a short poem Rosalie had just taught her about decorum. Rosalie paced slowly along the floor, despite her desire to leap for joy. There would be time enough for praise and reward later. For that moment, she could not distract her young pupil, no matter how thrilled she was at Sophia having learned the poem so quickly.

"Once more, Sophia," she said, her excitement slipping into her voice.

Sophia must have heard it, as she grinned and sat up straighter.

"It's fine to say how you do, but these things you must never do," she said, taking a deep breath. "Never shout or interrupt, and one can never be abrupt. Fold your hands and hold tight your knees, and you will be as proper as they please."

Rosalie applauded the child, grinning, as she had been longing to. Princess, who had been sitting obediently beside Sophia's chair throughout the morning's lessons, reacted to the happiness in the room by jumping up and putting her paws on the girl's lap. Sophia petted her briefly, before gently ordering the dog to sit back down.

"Very well done," Rosalie said. "You learned that so quickly, Sophia."

The girl smiled proudly.

"None of my other governesses ever helped me learn things through poems," she said. "I had so much fun learning it that way."

Rosalie nodded wisely.

"That was the point, Sophia," she said. "And now, I believe we can have even more fun. In fact, I believe I owe you my end of our bargain."

Sophia squealed with delight.

"Do you mean we can go outside?" she asked.

Rosalie nodded again.

"We certainly can," she said. "You learned all your decorum lessons perfectly this morning. And you did exceptionally well, despite how little you like those lessons. I am very proud of you. So now, we can go out to the garden, just as I promised."

Sophia jumped up and down.

"Can we have a picnic together?" she asked. "It is noon now, after all."

Rosalie grinned.

"I think that sounds like a lovely idea," she said. "In fact, wait here, and I will arrange for a picnic basket with the cook."

Sophia giggled and clapped again.

"I am so excited," she said.

Rosalie stepped out into the hallway, instantly running into Beth. The housekeeper smiled warmly at her.

"Good day, Miss Stewart," she said. "You look to me in much better spirits."

Rosalie nodded, grinning.

"Sophia is a wonderful pupil," she gushed. "In fact, I was just about to go ask the cook if we might have a picnic prepared for lunch."

Beth patted her shoulders gently.

"Please, allow me to speak with the cook," she said. Her smile was kind, and her eyes told Rosalie what her lips did not. She wanted to spare Rosalie the embarrassment of facing the cook alone, as Beth knew how cruel the rest of the servants had been to her.

Rosalie nodded gratefully.

"You are so kind," she said. "Thank you so much. But only if you start calling me Rosalie. We are both employees, after all."

Beth's grin widened, and she nodded.

"Rosalie, then," she said. "I shall speak to the cook straightaway."

Rosalie followed behind the housekeeper, waiting just around the corner from the kitchens as Beth went in and requested the picnic basket. She thought about how fortunate she was to have one woman there whom she could see would quickly become her friend, and that Sophia seemed to enjoy her company, despite her governess's hideous deformity.

For the moment, the judgmental glares of Irene and Lady Olivia were forgotten, and Rosalie allowed herself to begin feeling comfortable in her new accommodations.

Beth returned a short time later with a large picnic basket filled with bread, cheese, sliced beef, and cakes.

"There you are," she said, handing the basket to Rosalie. "I should return to my duties now, but please let me know if you need anything else."

Rosalie squeezed the housekeeper's arm and smiled.

"Thank you again," she said.

As Beth went back down the long hallway, Rosalie went back upstairs. She went straight to the schoolroom, where Sophia was kneeling over something with her back to the door. When Rosalie entered, she could see the child hurriedly arranging something in another basket.

When she heard Rosalie, she quickly closed the basket and turned to face her, holding it out in front of her.

"May I bring this with us?" she asked.

Rosalie looked at her with curiosity. Perhaps she had gathered up some toys for Princess. Whatever the case, Sophia seemed so excited about the contents of the basket, and Rosalie saw no harm in granting the child her wish.

"Of course," she said. "Just be sure not to leave anything you bring outside."

Sophia grinned widely.

"Oh, I won't," she said.

Rosalie nodded, offering the girl her hand.

"Shall we, then?" she asked.

Sophia giggled, taking her hand with enthusiasm.

"Yes, we shall," she said, nearly dragging Rosalie from the room, Princess following right behind them.

They had just reached the hallway when two women stepped out just between them and the staircase. Rosalie curtseyed as she saw that it was Lady Livinwood and her daughter.

"Good day, Miss Stewart," the duchess said, smiling warmly at her and Sophia.

Lady Olivia's greeting was nothing more than a disdainful look that went completely unnoticed by her mother. Rosalie instantly felt insecure about her appearance, and she looked down at the floor, praying she could soon flee from Lady Olivia's hateful stare.

Sophia was oblivious to the tension, thankfully. She was smiling up at her grandmother, holding up her basket with one hand and pointing to the one Rosalie carried with the other.

"We are going to have a picnic outside," she announced. "We each have our own baskets."

Rosalie held her breath. She knew she should have spoken with the duchess about allowing Sophia to go outside during what was supposed to be lesson time. She hoped it would not upset Lady Livinwood that she had not asked permission beforehand.

The duchess nodded to her granddaughter. Rosalie waited for the questions she was sure were coming as she tried to read Lady Livinwood's face. She did not seem angry, but her face was turned toward Sophia, so she could not read her whole expression.

Then, Lady Olivia stepped forward, leaning down to meet Sophia's eyes and gave her a too-bright smile.

"Is that so?" she asked, flickering a glare at Rosalie before looking back at her niece. "What about your lessons?"

Rosalie began to feel frantic. Instantly, she knew the duchess's daughter sought to make trouble for her. If she confronted Rosalie in front of the duchess, she would hardly get a chance to defend herself. She knew the young woman would make sure of that.

Sophia seemed to be catching on to the tension between her aunt and her governess. She looked up at Rosalie, her happy expression beginning to falter. It gave Rosalie the will to muster up all her courage and look the duchess in the eyes, with the biggest smile she could manage.

"Sophia has done an excellent job with her lessons today, my lady," she said, making a point to not look at Lady Olivia as she spoke. "I simply thought that some time outside would be good for Sophia."

Lady Olivia's eyes widened in an exaggerated expression of bewilderment.

"Oh, dear," she said, feigning thoughtfulness, "but I thought Sophia has a few more lessons to get through today."

Rosalie's blood began to boil, but she kept smiling at the duchess.

"We will continue some of her lessons outside," she said with confidence. "Although she has finished all but one of them already today."

Rosalie could see Lady Olivia's mouth twitch, but the young woman held her expression. She said nothing more to Rosalie, however, choosing to turn to her mother and frown. She was pointedly trying to get the duchess's attention, but Lady Livinwood looked instead at Rosalie and Sophia and smiled.

"I am rather impressed to hear how quickly Sophia is grasping her lessons," she said sweetly. "And I must agree with you, Miss Stewart, I believe that spending time amid nature sounds like a marvelous idea."

Rosalie trembled with relief and triumph. As she curtseyed again to the duchess, she could feel Lady Olivia's hate-filled eyes boring right through her. She paid her no heed, however. Sophia's earlier cheery mood had returned, and she would do anything to ensure it stayed that way.

"Would you like to join us?" Sophia asked hopefully.

Rosalie's heart began to fall, until she realized the girl was only addressing her grandmother. Her aunt was staring angrily off into the distance, so she would not have known her niece had extended her the invitation, even if the girl had indeed done so.

The duchess shook her head, smiling sadly.

"Oh, my darling, I would love to be able to join you," she said with sincere regret in her voice, "however, I must see to the preparations for the house party. There is still much to do, and so little time. I am very sorry, dear."

Sophia looked a little crestfallen, but she smiled sweetly, nonetheless.

"It is all right, Grandmother," she said. "I understand. Perhaps you can join us the next time we have a picnic."

The duchess smiled warmly, both at her granddaughter and at Rosalie.

"That would be lovely," she said. She politely excused herself and, with a very irate looking Lady Olivia in tow, she disappeared down the hallway. The younger woman made a point to scowl furiously at Rosalie before vanishing with her mother. Rosalie did not realize she had sighed aloud until she felt Sophia's small hands slip into her own.

"Do not forget that Aunt Olivia is always in a bad mood, Miss Stewart," she said. Her smile was warm, but her eyes were concerned. "That is no reason why we cannot go enjoy our afternoon outside, is there?"

Rosalie looked down at the child, admiring her inner strength, and her love for her aunt, despite the woman's perpetually hateful disposition. Though she knew the real reason for Lady Olivia's cruelty, there was no reason for Sophia to see Rosalie upset by the young woman.

"You just might be the wisest person I know, Sophia," she said. "And you are absolutely correct. Come. Let us get to the lovely picnic that awaits us."

Chapter Ten

"Would you like to eat here, or would you like to go further into the garden?" Rosalie asked, looking down at the secondary basket Sophia was carrying. She had asked Rosalie if she could bring it, but she had not yet told her what was inside. She was terribly curious, but she allowed the child to keep her secret for the time being, as it seemed to make her very happy.

"Let us walk a bit further," she said, calling for Princess, who had fallen behind to chase a butterfly, to catch up to them.

Rosalie gestured for Sophia to lead the way, with Princess following right behind. They strolled past bushes with every color of rose imaginable blooming on them. Rosalie marveled as they walked, thinking how much like a storybook the Livinwood Manor gardens looked. There were benches and statues and water fountains around every corner, and Rosalie was immediately glad she had promised to bring Sophia out here sometimes as a reward for doing well at her lessons.

Suddenly, Sophia stopped, turning and zipping through the gardens, nearly losing Rosalie and Princess.

"Sophia?" Rosalie called, quickening her pace to catch up to the girl. "Where are you going?"

"Follow me," the child cried out, turning another corner, and disappearing.

For a moment, Rosalie's heart fell. When she made the same turn, Sophia was nowhere in sight. But she heard a giggle that, though muffled, sounded as though it was coming from right beside her. She took another step forward and saw an opening in the shrubs that led to the grassy field between the manor and the stables. There stood Sophia, laughing and pointing to a large oak tree not far away.

Rosalie laughed with relief, following the girl out of the gardens and toward the oak tree. As they drew closer, Rosalie could see that it was strong and lovely, with dense, rich green foliage, and beautifully shaped and kept branches. The shade it offered was immense, and the breeze created a sweet sound as it blew through the leaves.

"May we have our picnic here, Miss Stewart?" Sophia asked, breaking Rosalie out of her trance.

Rosalie nodded.

"I rather insist that we do," she said, still in awe.

Sophia grinned, picking up Princess and twirling her gently as Rosalie fetched the picnic blanket from the basket she was carrying and spread it out on the ground beneath the grand oak tree. Then, she reached for the basket to begin spreading out the food, when Sophia held out the basket she had been carrying.

"Open this one first, Miss Stewart," she said, giddy with whatever secret she was keeping.

Rosalie gave her a curious look.

"All right," she said, reaching for the basket.

Sophia held it open, vibrating with excitement as Rosalie reached into the basket. At first, she did not know what it was she was touching, until she felt crisp, fresh paper bound in leather. She gasped, pulling out a sketch book and turning it over in her hands.

"I saw how dreamy you looked when I talked about art and nature," Sophia said, shyness creeping into her voice. "I did not know what you would like to do best, so I brought a sketch book and some charcoals along with my paint, in case you wanted to draw instead."

Rosalie sighed happily as she stared at the book. It took her a moment to collect herself before she looked back up at Sophia.

"It has been many years since I sketched," she said.

Sophia frowned at her, confused.

"Why?" she asked. "Did you get bored of it?"

Rosalie shook her head. She was unsure of whether it was appropriate to tell Sophia about her father. But there was one other reason why she had not bothered to try to draw for so long.

"The last children I tutored were not very fond of art," she said. "That left me very little time to sketch, though I wished to."

Sophia looked shocked.

"How can anyone not like art?" she asked, clearly bewildered. "Even Papa likes art, though he is often too busy with work to enjoy it."

Rosalie shrugged.

"I do not understand how people can be uninterested in art either," she said. "I used to paint and sketch with my father when I was younger."

Sophia studied her for a minute, seeming to understand there was something about it that Rosalie wished not to discuss. Instead of asking more questions, she sat down on the blanket Rosalie had laid on the ground, patting the spot right beside her.

"Well, now, you can sketch and paint with me," she said, giving the governess a shy smile. "Would you like to do so now?"

Rosalie's lip trembled, and she bit it to keep the little girl from seeing it. After her father fell ill, they could not afford to buy new drawing materials. And after he died, she simply lost heart for it. She could, indeed, have made time and effort for sketching, had Lord and Lady Winsdale's children taken an interest in art. But since they did not, she'd focused on the usual lessons and foregone her artistic pleasures.

"Yes," she whispered, smiling at the young girl. "I would love to draw and paint with you. Thank you, Sophia."

Sophia motioned for her to sit beside her again, and Rosalie complied. She gingerly opened the sketch book, noting it had no drawings in it as yet. It looked as though it was brand new, and Rosalie was touched that the child would allow her to use something that she herself had not even used yet.

She put her hand back into the basket and pulled out a nice, also new, piece of charcoal, admiring it as she did so. Instantly, an image popped into her mind, as it always did when she was inspired, and she set to work at once.

She felt chills as she touched the charcoal to the page. She was immediately focused, drawing her lines with experience and finesse she was glad to see she had not lost. She was instantly filled with all the comfort and joy sketching had always brought her, and the picture seemed to put itself on the page, with little effort from her.

"It is a rose," Sophia said softly from beside her.

Rosalie looked at the girl, feeling the euphoria from the lingering trance. The picture was less than half finished, but she smiled at it with great glee and pride.

"You knew what it was straightaway," she said, smiling at the child. "You truly do have a good eye for art."

Sophia shook her head, pointing to the page over which Rosalie's hand still hovered with the charcoal.

"Perhaps," Sophia mused. "But it is easy to tell what you are drawing because you are really good at it."

Rosalie blushed. It had been so many years since anyone had told her that her art was good.

"Thank you, Sophia," she said. "But never underestimate your talent for knowing beautiful art when you see it."

Sophia nodded, but she was now looking at Princess, who was grooming herself nearby. She looked back and forth between the dog and Rosalie before grinning widely.

"Would you mind doing a sketch of Princess and I together?" she asked.

Rosalie was shocked. Apart from her father, no one had ever asked her to do a portrait of them, or any living being.

"It is 'Princess and me,'" she said automatically. "And I am not sure if I am good enough to draw both you and Princess."

Sophia raised her eyebrows and looked at Rosalie as though she was mad.

"Of course, you are," she said. "It is only partially finished, and I know that yours is the most beautiful rose I have ever seen. I just know that you will draw a perfect picture of Princess and *me*." She clasped her hands together and smiled proudly at having corrected herself.

Rosalie bit her lip, blushing from the praise. No one had ever said such kind things about her drawings besides her father. It was such a welcome contrast to the suffering she had endured because of her appearance. She looked at Princess, who suddenly realized that people were watching her, and she came bounding over, leaping into Sophia's lap and licking her face.

"Do you think Princess will sit still, even for a second?" she asked, laughing. "I am not quite sure how to go about drawing a moving dog."

Sophia giggled, watching as Princess scrambled out of her lap to crawl into Rosalie's, her belly up and her legs kicking.

"I think she will probably run off chasing butterflies," she said, laughing harder as the pug puppy began snorting with apparent indignance at not being patted immediately. "Would you please try to draw us, though? I promise to do my best to make her sit still with me. Please, Miss Stewart?"

Rosalie laughed. She knew Sophia was absolutely right. But the girl was so excited and hopeful about the prospect of Rosalie sketching her and her beloved pet. And truthfully, Rosalie relished the idea of drawing her pupil and the little pug pup. It would be a challenge, to be sure, but it would be wonderful to be able to sketch again.

"Very well," she said, much to the little girl's delight. "You and Princess sit there, on the blanket, and I shall sit in front of you to draw."

Sophia leapt for joy, embracing Rosalie tightly.

"Oh, thank you, Miss Stewart," she said. "I will do my very best to keep Princess with me, I promise."

Rosalie nodded.

"I know you will, dear," she said. Then, she picked a spot a few paces away from where Sophia sat coaxing the little pug to sit beside her. As Rosalie expected, that failed, and Sophia quickly became exasperated. But then, her face lit up, and she looked hopefully at Rosalie.

"May I take a piece of food from our picnic to offer Princess as a treat?" she asked.

Rosalie gasped and nodded.

"I cannot believe I did not think of that," she said, remembering what the child had told her about using meat from meals to train the puppy. "Yes, you certainly may."

Sophia immediately reached into the basket, carefully pulling out a slice of meat and breaking it into small pieces. Princess smelled it instantly and started climbing on Sophia to get the food. Sophia held all but a single bite above her head, looking sternly at the dog.

"Princess, sit," she said.

The dog, though antsy, sat down in the girl's lap. Sophia gave her the single bite, hiding the rest behind her when the animal was not looking. Princess licked Sophia's hands, then settled into her lap without difficulty.

"Very good," Rosalie said, impressed. "Are you ready for me to begin?"

Sophia beamed a bright smile and nodded.

"Ready," she said.

Rosalie nodded and began. She marveled first at how wonderful it felt to be drawing again. It felt like a missing piece of her heart had been returned to her, and she lost herself in the project. As she worked, she then began to marvel at how still and well-behaved Princess was being. It seemed that Sophia had indeed caught onto something by using morsels of meat to train the dog.

She promised herself that she, too, would try to slip some of the meat from her meals to Sophia, to help the girl further the animal's training.

She quickly made excellent progress with the drawing. Both the subjects sat like statues for quite some time, and Rosalie expected to finish the sketch within an hour or so. But then, as predicted, something caught Princess's attention. Sophia acted quickly, reaching behind her, moving as little as possible, to fetch another piece of meat.

However, Princess had forgotten about the treats Sophia had for her. Before either she or Rosalie could stop her, the dog bolted from the girl's lap and ran toward the manor, barking. And a moment later, Sophia disappeared, too.

Chapter Eleven

Cedric smiled to himself as he turned the horse he had ridden to Mr. Brown's into the driveway of his family's mansion. The impromptu meeting with the man had gone well, much better than he had expected when he left Mr. James earlier.

The farmer had been polite and apologetic and had assured him he would make the rent payments within a fortnight. Cedric felt confident that any discrepancies with the other tenants were merely a coincidence, and that he had resolved the issue in a way that would have made his father proud.

He was whistling softly to himself, and was almost at the front door, when he heard a familiar bark. Princess was running up to him at full speed, so he brought the horse to an immediate stop. He dismounted, bending down to pet the excited dog before she jumped up on his pants. When he looked up again, he saw Sophia running toward them, clearly in pursuit of the animal. And yet, there was no adult accompanying her.

"Why are you not in your lessons?" he asked. "And why are you out here by yourself?"

His daughter did not answer him straightaway. Instead, she stood up straight, with perfect posture and, in a voice more confident than he could ever remember hearing from her, recited a poem to him. It did not sound familiar to him, though he had to admit he was impressed. It sounded as though it was about proper decorum, so he listened intently to the short recital.

"Miss Stewart taught me that," she said, answering his next question before he asked it. "She is teaching so many things. And she promised that if I did well in my lessons, we could spend some time outside. And I have done well, Papa."

Cedric knelt down and kissed his daughter on the cheek.

"You certainly have, darling," he said. "But where is Miss Stewart?"

Sophia turned to point just as Cedric heard rustling skirts. A moment later, a flustered looking governess appeared. Her eyes were wide with concern, but she did not look angry, as many of Sophia's governesses often had. Relief flooded her face, but only for a moment, before she saw that Cedric was standing beside his daughter.

Immediately, she dipped into a curtsey, and he realized suddenly that she was probably the author of the poem she had taught his daughter. She truly was a good governess, and it seemed Sophia enjoyed her time with Miss Stewart, too. And it did no harm that she was pretty, as well.

They locked eyes, and Cedric found himself once more mesmerized by her green eyes. For a moment, nothing existed except for the two of them. He still could not see the rest of her face for her bonnet, but he did not need to. He could stare into her eyes of the most perfect jade-green he had ever seen for all of eternity.

Too late, he realized he had been staring at her for far too long. It was not until Sophia spoke, a bit too loudly, that he remembered himself and looked away with great reluctance.

"Papa," Sophia said, pulling her father's attention to her. "Would you like to join us for our picnic?"

Cedric glanced at the governess, then back at his daughter. He had more work to do, he knew, but he had never been able to say no to his daughter.

"I would love to join you," he said, bending to offer Sophia his arm. "Lead the way."

The girl squealed with delight as she took it, pulling her father toward the governess. When she reached the woman, she linked her free arm through Miss Stewart's, who smiled down fondly at Sophia. Cedric marveled at her warmth and admitted secretly to himself that he was glad for the opportunity to get to know the young woman better.

It had been bold of her to presume to bring Sophia outside during what was supposed to be her lesson time. But the fact that she cared enough about Sophia to put her needs and desires first was intriguing to him. In that spirit, he gave her a small smile, even though she was looking at his daughter and did not see it and followed them quietly to their little picnic spot under the large oak tree at the back of the manor.

The governess immediately set up the picnic when they reached the shade beneath the grand tree. The feast looked delicious, and Cedric was glad he had chosen to take the time away from work to eat with them.

Sophia helped Miss Stewart set things out, and Cedric marveled at the way the governess taught his daughter proper table setting etiquette, even during a picnic. It reinforced the notion that she knew what she was doing by allowing Sophia time outside, and he smiled at the pair again.

"You seem to be a very good pupil, Sophia," he said, stroking her hair gently.

Sophia beamed at him again.

"I am, Papa," she said proudly. Cedric, too, was proud to see his daughter so confident and happy. Whatever Miss Stewart was doing was working wonders for his little girl. And the woman herself seemed very loving and kind. For that, he was grateful.

As they ate, Sophia talked about her other lessons, with Miss Stewart helping her to explain things that she struggled yet to understand. The governess also gently corrected her a couple of times when she made grammar mistakes, and Sophia took the criticism with grace and gratitude.

Cedric was impressed at how well Sophia was getting on in her lessons in such a short time, and he made a mental note to speak with his mother about the progress and the changes in his daughter.

"Did you know that Miss Stewart is really good at sketching, Papa?" Sophia asked, finishing the last bite of the cakes the governess had served to her.

Cedric looked at his daughter with genuine surprise. He did not know the governess was accomplished in art. Her last governesses had all seemed very uninterested in the subject, so he had never considered whether Miss Stewart might enjoy it or not.

"Is she, now?" he asked, smiling at his daughter. "I imagine you like that very much, darling."

Sophia nodded.

"I am so glad she shares my love of art, Papa," she said. "And she makes all my lessons seem easy and fun. She even lets me come out here when I do well. She is the best governess ever."

Cedric nodded, listening to his daughter as he stared at the young governess. She was very focused on her task of tidying up, so he had a minute to look at her properly. He still could not see much of her face, as her bonnet was pulled, as ever, strategically over it. But he got glimpses of the heart shape of her lips, her small, delicate nose, and her high, dainty cheekbones.

Suddenly, she reached for something on the other side of the picnic basket. When she pulled back, her bonnet, which came undone, slipped from its rigid position, exposing nearly the entirety of her face. It took him a moment to notice, as he was enraptured by the glimpses of her eyes he could see. But when he did, he studied her all the harder.

She had a big birthmark on her cheek, and it was completely visible to him. Against her pale skin, it was a stark contrast, and he found it most endearing. She continued working without a care in the world, and Cedric realized instantly that she was utterly oblivious to the fact that her face was exposed. He could see her every feature, and he knew then that she was, indeed, exquisitely beautiful.

"Papa," Sophia whispered, pulling his face toward hers. "Please, do not stare at Miss Stewart. It makes her feel really awful when people do that and are mean to her. Just as it does me."

Cedric patted his daughter's cheek.

"I have no intention in the world of being mean to her, darling," he said, glancing at the governess again, his smile returning. "I could never imagine doing such a thing."

Sophia looked over at her governess, and then back at her father.

"I think she might feel nice if you tell her how pretty she is," she said, her whisper becoming quieter.

Cedric shook his head gently at the child.

"I cannot do such a thing, Sophia," he said, pointing to the book that sat abandoned behind the governess. "What is that?"

Sophia followed his finger, smiling when she saw that book. She explained to him that it was the book containing Miss Stewart's drawings.

Cedric smiled again, flushing as he once more took in the loveliness of Miss Rosalie Stewart. He moved over closer to her, pointing to the sketch book his daughter had professed to have given to the governess. He could not, in fact, tell the governess how pretty she was, no matter how true it happened to be. He could, however, find a way to give her some of the praise she so clearly deserved.

"May I see it?" he asked.

Chapter Twelve

"I do hope it is all right that I've joined you both for your picnic, Miss Stewart," the duke said, gazing at her over his daughter's head.

Rosalie glanced at him, giving him a tight smile.

"Of course, Your Grace," she lied. "It has been a lovely afternoon."

The duke nodded, listening as Sophia told him more about her lessons. Rosalie tried to repress the knot of awkward discomfort that formed in her stomach. He was a nice enough employer, but she could not be herself in his company.

On top of her insecurities about her appearance, he was incredibly handsome, and she always felt flustered in his presence. She knew such thoughts were inappropriate, as she was his employee, and well below his station as duke. But when he looked at her in the way he had moments before, she could not help but feel attracted to him.

Her unease soon gave way, however, as she watched the duke with Sophia. It was very clear to her that the duke was very invested in his daughter, and that was rare within high society and nobility. Most titled gentlemen could not be bothered to spend time with their children, especially not their daughters.

But more than that was the fact that the duke did not seem troubled or uncomfortable with his daughter's deformity. Having one blue and one brown eye would make it far less likely for her to be accepted within the *ton*. And yet the duke clearly adored his daughter without reserve and greatly enjoyed her company.

Rosalie could not help thinking of her own father. He had loved spending time with her, and they did practically everything together when he was alive. But that was common practice for people of her family's class, as they did not have servants, nursemaids, and governesses. But Rosalie had been closer still to her father because of her mother's absence in her life, and it touched her heart to see a nobleman who appeared to be just as close with his daughter.

Her sketchbook, which she had carelessly tossed aside when Sophia ran after Princess, was not mentioned until after they had finished their meal. As she gathered up the plates to put back in the basket, she heard Sophia talking to her father about their afternoon of sketching.

Vaguely she heard the duke ask about what they had been working on that afternoon. Not until it was too late did she realize he was asking his daughter about the book in which she had been drawing.

"That is Miss Stewart's sketch book," Sophia said, beaming at Rosalie. "I gave it to her when we came out here for our picnic. She is very talented at sketching, Papa."

Rosalie smiled at the child gushing to her father about Rosalie's drawings, and how good she thought Rosalie was. However, the familiar self-consciousness crept back in, clenching her stomach, and she avoided looking at them as she finished clearing up. There was a silence that seemed to stretch on forever to Rosalie, and she wished the duke had never joined their picnic.

To her dismay, the duke moved toward her and pointed to the sketch book, looking at her with curiosity.

"May I see it?" he asked, giving her a warm, crooked smile.

Rosalie's heart leapt into her throat. She tried to will herself to speak, but her mouth was frozen closed. She could hardly deny him, but she was terribly modest about her work. She was surprised to learn that the child had gifted her the book, and she would be sure to thank her later. But first, she had to answer her employer, who was looking at her with curious expectancy.

As though sensing her hesitation, Sophia ran over and hugged her tightly.

"I believe you are the best artist I have ever seen," she whispered before turning back to her father. "You will see, Papa. She is very good."

Rosalie took a deep breath. She could not put off her employer any longer. She gave him a tight, pained smile and nodded.

"Of course, you may look, Your Grace," she said, feeling her cheeks flush.

She was all too happy to look away from him to reach for the book. Reluctantly, she held it out to him, her heartbeat roaring in her ears. She was so nervous that she did not see when his hand grasped the book, but she felt it when his fingers brushed hers. Thrills of awareness coursed through her, and the flush in her cheeks deepened. She looked into his eyes for a moment before turning shyly away.

From the corner of her eye, she watched him survey her half-finished drawing of Sophia and Princess. He stared at it for so long that she felt an overwhelming urge to yank the book from his hands and flee. She held her breath, praying that he would hurry and close the book and tell her and Sophia to go back inside and get back to their lessons, just so her self-conscious agony would at last come to an end.

To her amazement, he looked up at her and smiled, his eyes filled with genuine wonder and kindness. She had to admit he had the most charming smile she had ever seen. And each time she saw it, it only affirmed the notion in her mind: Employer or not, he was handsome, and she could not help smiling back.

"Sophia was right, Miss Stewart," he said, softly closing the book and handing it back to her. "You are, indeed, a very talented artist. Did you study art with someone?"

Rosalie blushed more fiercely than ever before in her life. She shook her head, glancing away, too bashful to continue looking her employer in the eyes.

"No, Your Grace," she said. "But my father and I spent a great deal of time drawing and painting. I suppose I just learned from him."

The duke studied the drawing again, for some time, then looked back at her again.

"I truly do not think I have ever seen such skill, even from people who have hired the finest art tutors," he said. "You have a rare gift. You should be very proud."

Rosalie felt she might swoon with such praise. She fumbled desperately for words to express her gratitude. But the way he looked at her made it near impossible for her to speak a word. She cursed her self-conscious, shy nature. It would take her ages to simply thank her employer for his kind words.

Before she could summon the words, the sound of an approaching carriage interrupted the moment. The duke looked at her for a moment longer, his eyes seeming to travel over her entire face. Then, he suddenly rose, straightening his suit and bowing to Rosalie and Sophia.

"I am afraid I must go and tend to the guests," he said abruptly. "I hope you both enjoy the rest of your afternoon."

After kissing Sophia quickly atop her head, the duke turned and hurried back toward the manor. Rosalie watched him walk away, her mind still reeling from his kind words and the way she had felt when their fingers touched.

Deep down, she hated the arriving carriage. Had it not been for that, she could have spent more time with the duke. Inappropriate though it may be, she now found she greatly enjoyed being in his company, and he gave her constant butterflies.

She had turned back to the picnic area when Sophia scooted over to her. She blushed, foolishly fearing the girl could read her thoughts. With a firm mental shake, she smiled at the child.

"Did you enjoy our picnic, Sophia?" she asked.

The girl nodded happily.

"It was the loveliest picnic I have ever attended," she said.

Rosalie smiled, preparing to stand and fold up the blanket, so they could return to the schoolroom. But before she could, Sophia cupped the governess's face in her tiny, cool hands.

"Miss Stewart," she said, looking at Rosalie with affectionate sincerity. "You are very pretty. I just wanted to be sure to tell you that."

Rosalie's flush returned with a fierceness, and she smiled fondly at the girl. Then horror struck Rosalie. The child had her bare hands placed on Rosalie's bare cheeks. That would only be possible if her bonnet was no longer fastened and snug on her face.

She resisted the urge to push the child's hands away and tighten the bonnet. The last thing she wanted was to make Sophia feel bad when she was only trying to give Rosalie a genuine compliment and make her feel happy.

But the horror would not leave her heart. Her loose bonnet meant that the duke had seen her face completely exposed. There could be no doubt that he had seen her hideous deformity. She would never forgive herself for being so careless as to allow the bonnet to slip without her realizing it. But she could not let the young girl still holding her face see her react with complete shame. She smiled, despite her stomach twisting itself into knots and threatening to expel the lovely lunch she had just had.

"Thank you for your kind words, Sophia," she said gently. "And I think that you are very pretty, too."

Sophia's eyes lit up, and Rosalie could not help smiling.

"Thank you, Miss Stewart," she said.

Rosalie nodded.

"Would you like to help me finish gathering everything, so we can return to the manor now?"

Sophia nodded, seeming hardly fazed that their time outside was now ended. Immediately, she set to work putting away all the art supplies in her basket, while Rosalie folded up the blanket and checked to make sure she had not left any food or plates lying unattended nearby. When she was satisfied she had collected everything, she tucked the blanket beneath her arm and waited for Sophia to finish.

She saw Sophia had already neatly packed up the basket she brought and was playing with Princess while Rosalie finished. She pretended to work a little longer to give the child a few extra minutes in the garden. She used the chance to collect her thoughts. She still felt embarrassed at having had her face exposed.

The duke had seen it; she had seen it in his eyes. And then the carriage arrived, after which he seemed happy to take his leave. Could he have used the carriage as an excuse to flee?

Chapter Thirteen

Cedric rushed toward the arriving carriage, relieved for the interruption. He'd had a wonderful picnic with Sophia and the governess, but it had stirred feelings within him that he was not yet prepared to handle. It reminded him of what it was like to have a woman in his life, which was something he had sworn to forget.

It also made him realize that he found Miss Stewart very attractive, despite the birth mark on her cheek. He wondered if that was the reason why she was so kind to Sophia, and why Sophia had become attached to her so quickly. It was irrelevant to him, however. To him, both Sophia and Miss Stewart were very beautiful.

As he continued toward the carriage, he scolded himself for such thoughts. No nobleman should ever have such thoughts about his employees. It was inappropriate and scandalous. It was acceptable for him to appreciate the governess for her kindness and skill with his daughter.

But that was far as any interactions between them could ever go, and he would do well to remember that. Perplexed, and more than a little confused, Cedric hurried to the front of the manor. He tried to shake off such thoughts and compose himself

As he turned the corner, he saw the carriage just stopping in front of the front door. Before its passenger saw him, he spotted a familiar crest on the back of the coach. He approached just in time to see his good friend, Edgar, alight from the carriage.

"I trust you know the front door is right there," Edgar said, grinning and pointing as Cedric approached. "There was no need to use the servant's entrance just to greet me."

Cedric sneered in jest at his friend as he shook his hand.

"I trust you know that tomorrow is not today," he retorted with a chuckle. "Or do you have as poor of a memory as you do wit and humor?"

Edgar laughed heartily.

"I am aware that today is today," he said. "I just thought I would test you, to see if you do." He guffawed again as Cedric rolled his eyes. Then, he cleared his throat and became marginally more serious. "I hope you do not mind that we have arrived a day early for the party."

Cedric shook his head.

"I do not mind at all," he said, raising an eyebrow. "Though it is a little strange. You are hardly well known for your punctuality."

Edgar laughed.

"I am full of surprises," he said, winking.

Cedric snorted.

"That, you are," he said. "Where is your sister?"

Just then, a young woman, wearing an expression of playful annoyance, poked her head out of the open coach door.

"Are you going to help me out with this thing?" she asked sharply.

Edgar laughed again, walking over, and taking the young woman's hand.

For a moment, Cedric did not recognize her, and he looked at his friend expectantly. Edgar was quick with his reaction, putting a hand on Cedric's shoulder.

"Cedric, you remember my sister, Isabel," he said.

Recognition flooded Cedric, and he could not help staring. He had known Isabel almost as long as he had known Cedric, but she had gone to live with her aunt six years prior, and he had not seen her since. He could hardly believe how much she had changed.

When last he saw her, she was a young teenage girl with mousy hair and a temper as big as his manor. But before him now stood a lovely, mature young lady.

To further his surprise, she curtseyed to him as her brother reintroduced the pair. He bowed, smiling kindly at her.

"It is lovely to see you again, Lady Isabel," he said.

Her face lit up as she returned his smile.

"Likewise, Your Grace," she said.

Edgar looked pointedly at Cedric, glancing toward the manor.

"Well, do you plan to invite us inside?" he asked, pretending to be annoyed. "Or will we be sleeping here with the wildlife during our stay?"

Cedric glared at his friend, but he smiled as he began leading them to the door.

"*You* just might be, Edgar," he said. "Go on and try me, if you like."

Edgar's sister folded her arms crossly, but Cedric knew she was resisting a smirk.

"If I didn't know better, I would believe that I was standing here with a couple of schoolboys," she said.

Edgar grinned slyly.

"I know there is one schoolboy out here," he said. "And his name is not Edgar."

Cedric rolled his eyes again.

"Let us go inside, before I am forced to show you which of us is childish," he said. "And his name is not Edgar."

The three of them laughed as they approached the door, which was being held open by the butler.

"Where are Mother and Olivia?" Cedric asked the man as he motioned for his guests to enter the manor.

The butler glanced down the hallway, frowning.

"They were right behind me just now, milord," he said, pointing down the hall. "They were accompanying me to the door to receive the guests."

Cedric nodded.

"Thank you," he said. "You may return to your duties."

The butler bowed, excusing himself from Cedric and his guests. Cedric beckoned for Edgar to follow him down the hallway in the direction where the butler had pointed. He figured that, if nothing else, his parents would have lingered in the drawing room to wait for the butler to announce Edgar and Lady Isabel.

He and his friend continued to banter back and forth as they had outside. It had been some time since Edgar had been to see him at his manor, and little had changed. In fact, little had changed since they were young men and his father had still been alive. It felt a bit like returning to his younger years to have Edgar in his home, and he found he was glad that his friend had arrived a day early for the party.

Cedric was so engaged in his repartee with Edgar that he almost ran straight into someone who was hurriedly approaching them. He scowled, looking down in preparation to chastise a rushing servant. He blinked and stepped back, however, when he found himself looking into the smiling face of his sister.

"Well, that solves a mystery," he said, baffled. "Where is Mother?"

Olivia looked past him toward Edgar and Isabel.

"Oh, she is just along here," she said, gesturing to somewhere vaguely behind her. "Are you not going to introduce me, Brother?"

Cedric raised an eyebrow, but he complied. He formally reintroduced his sister to his friend and Isabel. Olivia gave them a graceful, elegant curtsey, and her smile brightened.

"Oh, of course," she said sweetly. "I remember both of you well. It is so lovely to see you again."

Cedric had to bite his lip to keep his mouth closed. Olivia was known to be moody on the best of days. But just then, he was witnessing her being downright friendly. And dare he say, charming? He looked at Edgar and Isabel to gauge their reactions to Olivia, but each bowed and curtsied, respectively, and warmly returned the greeting.

Mother would swoon if she saw Olivia now, he thought to himself, hiding a chuckle with a feigned cough. Edgar shot him a questioning look, but Olivia was too oblivious to notice. Cedric allowed the trio to talk, finding the butler once more and fetching him for when they felt sufficiently caught up.

"Would you like some refreshments after your trip?" Cedric asked, watching his sister's polite demeanor and decorum with surprise as she kept them engaged in light conversation.

Edgar glanced at Isabel, then looked back at Cedric.

"That was, indeed, a long trip," he said. "I think we should have a rest before dinner tonight, if that is all right."

Cedric bowed, nodding his consent.

"Of course, it is," he said. "And Edgar, I have decided that you may have a room inside, after all. The butler will take you up to your rooms as soon as you are ready. Any more shenanigans, however, and it is straight to the stables with you."

Edgar grinned, puffing out his chest.

"I will be the model of bad etiquette, my friend," he said.

Olivia giggled wildly at the joke, and Cedric once more marveled at her disposition. Perhaps seeing old friends was lifting her spirits. He made a mental note to suggest to their mother that the three women spend some time together planning for the party the following evening or having tea in the gardens. She would surely not believe the change in Olivia until she saw it herself, and he wanted to be sure she did.

After another moment, Edgar and Isabel excused themselves, promising to be fresh in time for dinner that evening. Olivia stood beside Cedric, watching as they followed the butler up the stairs.

"I cannot remember the last time I saw you smile this way, Sister," Cedric said, patting Olivia on the shoulder.

Olivia grinned sweetly at him, kissing him on the cheek.

"I hope you can get accustomed to it," she said before skipping back down the hall.

Baffled, Cedric watched until his sister disappeared. Then, he went to his study to tend to some long-postponed ledgers.

Chapter Fourteen

Rosalie was awakened the following day by a rapturous pounding on her door. For a moment, she was disoriented, and she tripped out of bed and stumbled to the door. It was not until she saw the face on the other side that she was brought round to full alertness.

"Miss Stewart," Irene hissed, her expression ever sullen. "Are you aware of the time?"

Rosalie shook her head, but the tall clock in the hallway told her the answer. It was eight o'clock in the morning.

"Oh, dear," she said, but Irene held up her hand.

"Dress yourself, and hurry to the schoolroom," she said, her voice still venomous. "Miss Sophia is already dressed and waiting to start her lessons."

Irene turned on her heel and stormed away, but Rosalie had nothing to say to her anyway. Fear raced through her body as she hurriedly dressed and tidied her hair. She could not believe she'd overslept, and she had no excuse for having done so. She had no time for breakfast, but the growing dread in her stomach left no room for food anyway.

As soon as she was presentable, she hurried out of her room and down the passageway. The only thought in her head was of the potential for being dismissed for her blunder. The dread twisted her stomach into a knot as she thought of the possibility.

The chances of her finding another governess position was extremely slim. She could not afford another delay between positions, financially or mentally, and she could not return to Winsdale Manor for aid. If she lost this job, she would be headed straight for the poorhouse.

She was so distressed and lost in her thoughts that she was not watching where she was going. In her haste, she bumped straight into someone. Mortified, she looked up, and straight into the eyes of Lady Olivia. Chills ran down her spine as the young woman glared at her. She instinctively took a step back and gave her an awkward curtsey.

"My lady," she said, horrified and embarrassed. "Please, forgive me. I didn't mean to be so careless. I am truly sorry for running into you."

She had not expected kindness from the woman. In fact, she hoped to be largely ignored, once she moved away from the woman. But instead, Lady Olivia sneered at her, putting her hands on her hips, and blocking Rosalie's path.

"I am onto the game you are playing," she said.

Rosalie gaped at her, utterly confused, and flustered.

"Game?" she echoed. "I do not understand what you mean."

Olivia shook her head, wagging a finger in the air.

"It is no use denying it or feigning daftness, governess," she said. "I happened to spot you having a picnic with my brother and my niece yesterday. Your little plot will fail, I can assure you."

Rosalie shook her head, more baffled than before.

"Sophia asked her father to join us for our picnic," she said, uncertain of why she was defending herself. "I do not understand why you say I am playing a game."

Olivia snorted.

"Do not play coy with me," she said. "You would do well to stay away from my brother."

Rosalie wanted to cry as she stared into Lady Olivia's hate filled eyes.

"I am not sure how I could go about avoiding him, as he is the one who pays me," she said, wishing she sounded more indignant than like a scolded child.

Lady Olivia smirked.

"I think you and I both know what I mean, Miss Stewart," she said. "And in case you don't, I will tell it to you this way. My brother would never look at someone as hideous as you in a romantic way. Really, you would be doing yourself a favor if you remembered that."

Rosalie's mouth fell open, and she stared at Lady Olivia utterly speechless. Sophia had told her that her aunt was often in a bad mood, but her bitter words were outright malicious. If words could kill a person, Rosalie knew that she would have been lying dead on the floor rather than looking horrified at the young woman. How could she ever say such things to someone with a physical deformity, when her own niece suffered a similar affliction?

Lady Olivia seemed triumphant at Rosalie's silence. She returned to her original sneer, picking up her skirts and stomping her foot.

"You have wasted enough of my time, governess," she said. "Excuse me."

With that, the young woman stormed off, leaving Rosalie trembling in her wake. She held onto the wall until she once more had control of her knees. Only when she went to put her cool hands on her hot cheeks did she realize she was crying. She did not understand the animosity Lady Olivia had toward her.

She was hardly any competition for the duke's attention at all since she was a mere governess. Why had the young woman felt it so necessary to rip apart the tenuous self-esteem she had been building with Sophia's and the duchess's kindness?

Hurriedly, she wiped her face with her handkerchief and then stuffed it back into her pocket as she made the rest of the way to the schoolroom. She forced a smile as she entered the room, feeling her stomach knot once more when she saw the duchess engaged in a very animated conversation with Sophia. She was sure she would be dismissed if the duchess was waiting to speak with her.

The duchess noticed her in the doorway and looked up at her. She gazed straight at Rosalie's face, which she knew must look suspiciously like she had been crying, so she curtseyed quickly, praying that Lady Livinwood would not notice.

"Good day, Miss Stewart," the duchess said. Her tone was not sharp, but it was hard to read for Rosalie, with her raw nerves and her blood rushing in her ears. For a moment, Rosalie feared she would swoon from the exhaustion and emotional tension of the morning. Briefly, she hoped she would. At least she could avoid termination for a day or two while recovering from such a spell.

"Please, forgive me, Lady Livinwood," she said, her voice trembling. "I didn't mean to sleep in and run late for Sophia's lessons this morning. I can assure you that it will not happen again."

The duchess rose, and Rosalie held her breath. To her surprise, the duchess smiled sweetly and waved a gentle hand.

"Please, dear, do not fret," she said, walking over to Rosalie and putting her hands on the governess's shoulders. "I understand that working for us is an adjustment for you. You are doing a wonderful job, Miss Stewart. These things happen sometimes. You needn't worry, I assure you."

Rosalie felt her lip tremble, this time with relief. She was taken aback by the duchess's kindness and understanding, especially after the ugly confrontation with Lady Olivia. It made her emotional, but in a positive way, and it was all she could do to not embrace the kind woman.

Instead, she straightened herself and smoothed her dress, giving her a true, genuine smile.

"You are so kind, my lady," she said, curtseying again. "I shall not make you regret your leniency."

The duchess waved her hand again.

"You really must not fret," she said. "There are worse things you could do than sleep late once in a while."

Rosalie nodded, letting her relief and the duchess's warmth replace all the horror she had experienced with Lady Olivia.

"Thank you, just the same, my lady," she said.

The duchess nodded, dipping her head gracefully.

"Now, I shall leave the two of you to it," she said. "I must prepare for our guests. They will begin arriving any time now."

She walked back over to Sophia and kissed her on the head.

"Be on your best behavior, and do well with your lessons again today, darling," she said. Then, she turned and smiled once more at Rosalie.

"And do not worry about any methods you choose to help Sophia with her studies," she said with a wink. "I assure you that my son and I trust your judgment implicitly."

With that, she left the room. Rosalie's head was spinning, and she walked to the front of the room to gather her materials along with her thoughts.

"What did she mean, Miss Stewart?" Sophia asked.

Rosalie turned around, a sly smile spreading across her face.

"She meant that you and I can continue spending time outside, if you do well in your lessons," she said.

Sophia's face lit up in that special way that made Rosalie's heart sing.

"Can we go right now?" she asked, putting her hands together in a pleading gesture.

Rosalie giggled.

"Not just yet, darling," she said. "But if you do well with your etiquette lessons, then we can go."

Sophia thought it over for a moment.

"Can you make it fun, like you did my last decorum lesson?" she asked hopefully.

Rosalie shrugged.

"If you will bear with me, we shall see," she said mysteriously.

Sophia nodded vigorously.

"I trust you," she said. "We have another deal."

Rosalie got through the tough, boring parts of the lesson as quickly as she could. She had Sophia write some phrases on the blackboard and made her recite the meanings of the phrases and when she was to use them. But then, she found a practical but fun exercise to help Sophia learn the proper way to behave during tea. She went to find Beth, who gladly brought her some pewter cups from the servant's quarter's kitchen and a pitcher of water. Rosalie promised to clean up any mess when their lessons were done.

For about an hour or so, Rosalie helped Sophia practice how to sit with perfect posture, by balancing a book on her head, and taking small sips from the cups filled with water.

Sophia thought it great fun to try to sit perfectly still, so that the book did not fall, and she giggled uncontrollably when it did. But by the end of the lesson, she could have a nice, polite conversation with Rosalie and sip her pretend tea properly, while the book did not budge a bit.

Last for the day was learning a proper curtsey. Rosalie made sure to impress upon her how important a good curtsey was, especially when meeting people for the first time, or when greeting anyone except for good friends at social events. She showed Sophia how to do a graceful curtsey a few times first before urging her to try.

Rosalie hid a giggle behind her hand as Sophia teetered in the middle of her curtsey. The girl was concentrating very hard, so hard, in fact, that Rosalie thought it was making her nervous. So, Rosalie had an idea.

"Let us skip and sing for a few minutes," she said.

Sophia straightened herself, so quickly she nearly toppled over, and looked at Rosalie dubiously.

"Skip and sing?" she asked. "In the middle of lessons?"

Rosalie winked at the girl.

"Trust me," she said. "This is to aid in our lessons."

Sophia studied her governess for another moment. Then, she shrugged.

"Very well," she said.

Rosalie skipped around gracefully in a small circle, humming a tune as she danced, to show the girl what she expected. Then, she twirled slowly, stopping to face the child, and dipping into a slow, deep curtsey. Sophia's face lit up, and she clapped her hands when Rosalie finished.

"It is a simple little dance step," Rosalie said. "Do you think you can do this with me?"

Sophia nodded, eagerly positioning herself beside Rosalie.

"I am ready," she said.

Rosalie nodded, humming the tune for a second before urging Sophia to join her in the skip and twirl. The first two times, the girl was giggling so hard that she could not keep her balance. Rosalie was indulgent with the child. She knew that children learned best when they felt comfortable and cared for.

And by the third and fourth time of the same exercise, Sophia had dramatically improved her technique. Well before the tenth time, she could do a flawless curtsey. And as soon as she realized what Rosalie had done, her eyes lit up and she grinned.

"Miss Stewart, look," she said, doing a perfect curtsey, without the skip and twirl.

Rosalie clapped her hands enthusiastically.

"Splendid," she said, still applauding. "Can you do it once more?"

Sophia nodded, standing with the perfect posture that Rosalie had taught her. Then, with a serious expression on her face, she dipped into a flawless curtsey. As she straightened herself, she too began clapping, her grin widening.

"That was so simple, Miss Stewart," she said. "I even had fun learning it."

Rosalie nodded knowingly.

"I suspected you would feel that way," she said. "And now, we can go outside."

Chapter Fifteen

"Oh, it will be simply wonderful," Cedric could hear his mother saying as he neared the main dining hall to join the duchess, Olivia, Edgar, and Isabel for breakfast. "I have hired the finest orchestra in London, and the cook is preparing a grand feast of roast duck and potatoes, with baked custard for dessert."

Cedric silently greeted everyone else at the table as his mother spoke before kissing her on the cheek before taking his seat.

"Good morning, Cedric," Edgar said, raising his cup of coffee in a toast. "I thought you might sleep all day."

Cedric rolled his eyes; it was just before ten o'clock.

"Would you have usurped my duchy if I had?" he asked, grinning.

Edgar's eyes grew amusingly wide, and he looked quickly around the table.

"He has discovered my plan," he said with a gasp. "I must flee."

Everyone, particularly the two women, burst into laughter.

"Edgar, you are mad," Isabel said, politely giggling behind her hand.

Cedric nodded his agreement.

"I shall send for the paddy wagon to fetch him," he said, taking up his fork as soon as his plate of food was served. "Right after I partake of these poached eggs."

Everyone laughed again, but the duchess was looking at him and his sister intently.

"The guests will likely begin arriving around noon," she said. "I trust you will both be ready to greet them and entertain them for tea."

Cedric winced, focusing on his meal rather than answering his mother. Olivia was very eager to reply, however.

"I am ready now, Mother," she said, seeming to exude pure self-pride. "I am so looking forward to dancing later this evening."

Cedric shuddered. He had always tried to avoid parties that involved dancing because he loathed it. But he was glad to know his sister was excited. If her mood remained pleasant, as it had been of late, she was sure to attract a good suitor. That put Cedric's mind a bit more at ease.

Throughout the meal, Cedric could not help noticing how Olivia batted her eyelashes at Edgar. He wondered if she had an interest in his friend, or if she was just seeking to have Edgar introduce her to some of the gentlemen he knew.

All he knew was that he was glad his sister seemed to be in good spirits. If that was any indication, he imagined she would do well in attracting suitors to her later that evening. Though he hated parties, he could find reasonable solace in helping his sister having a nice time.

After breakfast, Cedric invited Edgar to go riding. His friend happily accepted, and the gentlemen excused themselves from the women and left the manor together.

"It seems that our sisters struggle to remember one another," Edgar said.

Cedric shook his head.

"How do you mean?" he asked.

Edgar shrugged.

"They hardly spoke to each other," he said.

Cedric smiled wryly.

"Olivia has her mind focused on one thing," he said. "Please, do not let yourself or Lady Isabel take her demeanor too personally."

Edgar nodded slowly.

"She has grown into quite a lovely young woman," he remarked thoughtfully. "It is hard to believe that so many years have passed since we last visited you."

Cedric nodded, recalling his surprise at seeing Lady Isabel after so long.

"Your sister is quite grown up and mature, as well," he said. "Time is a strange thing. It seems as if it was just months ago when we were all young, immature, and foolish."

Edgar puffed out his chest and grinned.

"You do me a disservice," he said. "I am still young and immature."

Cedric surveyed his friend, snorting.

"You failed to mention foolishness, Edgar," he said. "That is, of course, the most important of all."

The two men laughed.

"Perhaps you could use a bit more laughter in your life, Cedric," Edgar said, studying him seriously for a moment. "Certainly, you could use more merriment."

Cedric shrugged.

"Would that I could experience more of it," he said.

Edgar patted him on the back.

"Perhaps the party tonight will be your chance to do just that," he said.

Cedric snorted again.

"Now you sound just like Mother," he said.

Edgar bellowed with laughter.

"Not quite," he said. "If I sounded like your mother, it would be something like this." He cleared his throat and proceeded to repeat what he had just said in a falsetto voice. Cedric doubled over with laughter, once more grateful that his friend had come to spend time with him. Though he was, indeed, less mature than Cedric himself, his heart was good, and his friendship was genuine.

"I suggest you take that routine to the theater and audition for the stage," Cedric teased.

Light, joyful laughter from a child rang in the air, disrupting their good-natured exchange. Cedric and Edgar both looked in the direction from whence the laughter came, and saw Sophia chasing after Princess, clearly filled with glee, with apparently not a care in the world. He smiled at his daughter, though she had not yet seen him, because her joy was infectious.

Yet something about seeing her so happy tugged at his heart. It was a rare sight for him, as she was usually so gloomy about her appearance. But to see her so happy was a staunch reminder that he had been rather selfish about not wanting to remarry.

He had let himself forget that Sophia might need a mother figure in her life. He had just taken for granted that his mother would be enough of a surrogate mother for her. But in his heart, he knew he was wrong in that assumption.

A shrill bark drew the attention of both the men. Cedric saw Princess, with her head swiveling over her shoulder every few bounds, running straight for them. Cedric's eyes widened. He did not want the dog to jump up on Edgar, as she was wont to do. But he was not quick enough to prevent the incident, and before he knew it, Princess was giving her usual greeting to Edgar.

His friend's laugh caught Cedric off guard. He watched as Edgar leaned down to pet Princess, cooing to her as one might an infant baby. He turned to Cedric; his eyes filled with warm curiosity.

"Where does this delightful pug come from?" he asked.

Cedric smiled.

"Her name is Princess," he said. "She belongs to my little Sophia. I did not know you had an affection for animals."

Edgar nodded.

"Oh, indeed," he said, scratching Princess under the chin and making her pant with pure joy. "I am very fond of dogs, especially. And Princess here is an instant heart winner."

Cedric sighed.

"She is precious," he said. "But I do hope that one day, Sophia can teach her to stop jumping on everyone that way."

"Princess," said Sophia, looking flustered and tired. "Come here this instant."

To his astonishment, the dog instantly obeyed. He watched as Sophia gave the instruction for the dog to sit down, and she complied. Then, Sophia looked back up and, seeing that her father was speaking with someone, she instantly dipped into a graceful curtsey. Then, she looked expectantly at her father, as though waiting for him to say something.

When Edgar cleared his throat, Cedric realized just what was expected of him. He quickly introduced Sophia to Edgar, trying to fight through his surprise to meet the formal expectations. If this was an exercise in helping Sophia practice her decorum, he wanted to be at his best.

"Good day, Viscount Burtondale," she said, smiling sweetly at Edgar. "I hope you are faring well."

Edgar looked at Cedric with intense approval before bowing to Sophia and returning her grin.

"I am well," he said. "It is a pleasure to meet you, Miss Sophia."

Sophia dipped her head, reminding him much of her mother.

"The pleasure is mine, Viscount Burtondale," she said, smiling.

Edgar chuckled.

"That is a fine dog you have there, Miss Sophia," he said.

Sophia smiled proudly.

"Thank you, Your Grace," she said, clasping her hands in front of her and holding herself with perfect posture. "I apologize for her jumping on you that way. I must work harder with her to ensure that she ceases such behavior."

Cedric and Edgar exchanged glances. Edgar's expression was clearly amused, but Cedric's was both bewildered and proud. He knew well that Sophia had struggled to grasp proper decorum. Yet it seemed as though she had learned everything a young lady needed to know in a matter of days. And she was speaking with such confidence too, despite her self-consciousness and insecurity about her eyes; that was the best surprise of all.

Cedric bent down to meet Sophia at eye level. He gave her a broad smile and a wink as he spoke to her.

"A blow," he said. "I must compliment you on your excellent decorum, Miss Sophia. To say that I am impressed would do you a great injustice."

Sophia beamed at him in a way that Cedric could not ever remember seeing. She looked every bit like the happy child he had always wished she could be.

"It is all thanks to Miss Stewart, Papa," she said. "Our lessons yesterday and today were about decorum and etiquette. And she makes learning those things such fun, and I never forget what she teaches me."

Cedric kissed his daughter on the cheek to mask his speechlessness. He already knew Miss Stewart was kind and smart, and that Sophia had taken a strong liking to her. But could one governess truly make such a difference with his daughter in just a matter of days?

As he opened his mouth to ask after the absent governess, the air around them was pierced by a bloodcurdling scream. Without hesitation, Cedric broke into a run in the direction of the sound.

Chapter Sixteen

It did not take long for Rosalie to lose sight of Sophia and Princess. She had a good idea of where Princess would be heading, so she went in that direction. She sighed heavily, understanding Irene's frustration on the first day Rosalie had encountered her.

Sophia knew not to run off, and yet she seemed to have a habit of doing just that. But she also should have been more focused on the girl and less so on her drawing.

As she reached the gentle crest of the hill, she saw Sophia standing with her father. But her stomach knotted when she saw the pair were not alone. There was another gentleman standing with them, and her nerves were instantly on edge. She dreaded the idea of having to engage with a stranger, especially if the duke was angry for having let Sophia get away from her.

Without looking, she took a step forward. She was not far from the trio, and they would see her soon enough. But instead of her foot hitting the ground, it sank through it. She only caught a glimpse of the rabbit hole into which she had stepped before she lost her balance and toppled toward the ground. Just as her body made a hard impact with the ground, she let out an ear-piercing scream.

Her ankle did not dislodge from the hole when she fell, and the pain in her left ankle was excruciating. She felt faint, unable to push herself up, keeping her eyes closed to try to combat a swoon. She believed she might black out, and she felt her cheeks flush with embarrassment, even as she struggled to remain conscious. The stranger would, no doubt, think her a clumsy, hideous beast. No doubt, she had just humiliated the duke, and poor Sophia, too.

"Are you all right?" said a concerned, baritone voice.

Rosalie recognized it as the duke's, and her heart skipped a beat. She forced herself to remain still and calm, though her pulse raced wildly. Her inner voice told her to keep her eyes closed, so she did so, careful to keep her eyelids from twitching or flickering.

Above her, she could hear the duke murmuring. She was unsure whether he was talking to himself or to the gentleman or Sophia. She remained motionless, wondering what the duke would do.

A pained sob pierced the air, and Rosalie realized that Sophia was standing right beside her father. The sound almost made her jump, but she willed her muscles to stay relaxed. But the child was inconsolable, making Rosalie think that she had somehow been hurt, too.

"Oh, Papa," Sophia wailed. "It is all my fault. I ran from Miss Stewart, even though I knew I was not supposed to, and she got hurt chasing me. I should never have run off and made her come after me."

Rosalie felt a vice grip tighten around her heart. The poor girl was terribly frightened and sad, and she could not allow Sophia's grief to continue. She opened her eyes slowly, and her heart stopped. Above her stood the duke, looking down at her with worry and fear. The fear seemed to melt when he saw her eyes were open, but the worry only deepened.

"Are you all right, Miss Stewart?" he asked, kneeling down and gently touching her forehead. "Can you hear me?"

Rosalie took a deep breath. Butterflies swirled in her stomach at his closeness, and, for a moment, nothing hurt. She tried to sit up, but searing pain shot through her left leg. She flinched, relaxing her body again, clenching her jaw to fight tears. Sophia had stopped sobbing when Rosalie opened her eyes. She did not want to upset the child and make her start crying again.

"I believe I might have hurt my ankle," she said, gingerly patting her left leg. "Please, forgive my clumsiness."

"No," Sophia said, more sternly than Rosalie would have ever expected from an eight-year-old girl. "It was not your fault, Miss Stewart. I should have never run from you. I knew better, and still I ran to chase Princess."

Rosalie turned her head and gave the girl a weak smile.

"You could not help Princess running off that way," she said. "She is still a young pup, and she will learn. But it is not your fault, darling."

The fresh tears filling Sophia's eyes slowly disappeared as dubious relief replaced them.

"Is there something I can do to help?" said a rich voice Rosalie did not recognize. She looked and saw the stranger with whom the duke and Sophia had been talking looking down at her with his eyebrows furrowed. Her eyes met his, and she felt her cheeks flush with embarrassment.

She was acutely aware that not only had she humiliated herself with her display, but she had also likely brought shame to the duke. She also knew there was nothing covering her face after that fall. She suddenly wished that the rabbit hole which had trapped her foot would swallow her whole.

While she was distracted with her self-loathing, the duke managed to get her foot free from the hole. She yelped, covering her mouth with her hand to muffle the sound. The duke gave her an apologetic smile before turning to the other gentleman.

"Yes, Edgar, as a matter of fact, there is," he said. "Please, go inside the manor and arrange for word to be sent to the physician straightaway."

The man nodded, dipping his head at Rosalie before turning and running to the manor. Rosalie felt more humiliated than ever, now that such fuss was being made over her. She tried once more to sit up, but the throbbing in her foot made it hard to focus on anything else. Sophia rushed to her, using all the strength in her tiny body to try to help Rosalie.

"Oh, Sophia, darling," she said, trying to smile at the girl through the pain. "You need not strain yourself to help me. It would not do for you to get hurt, as well."

Sophia stuck her chin in the air in a show of defiance, but her lip was trembling again, and her eyes were full of remorse.

"It is only fitting, after my behavior directly caused you such an injury," she said.

Rosalie's heart broke. She reached out and took Sophia's hand.

"You fulfilled your responsibility with Princess to the letter, darling," she said. "She ran from you, so you went after her, so that she could not get hurt or find trouble. You did nothing wrong. And we will discuss ways to teach Princess so that she does not run from you, and thus, you will not need to run from me. Deal?"

Sophia studied Rosalie's face, and she fought hard to keep all pain from her features. After a minute, Rosalie saw the ghost of the smile she had seen when making previous deals with Sophia, and the girl nodded.

"Deal," she said. "But only if you hurry and get better."

Rosalie smiled reassuringly at the child.

"I am sure this is nothing to worry about, Sophia, dear," she said. "I will be right as rain by tomorrow."

Sophia reluctantly backed away from Rosalie, but she stayed well within reach. Rosalie noticed that the duke was looking at her with a strange wonder in his eyes, paired with his still apparent concern. When he saw she was looking at him again, he shook his head and knelt beside Rosalie.

"It is all right," he said softly. "I have you."

Rosalie did not understand what was happening until the duke had swiftly lifted her off the ground. It caught her off guard, and she reflexively put her arms around his neck tightly.

He gave her a small smile and patted her back oh so gently.

"You are safe, Miss Stewart," he said, turning to take her toward the manor. "Please, trust in me."

Rosalie merely nodded, her racing heartbeat making her temporarily able to ignore the pain in her foot. The duke felt strong and secure to her, and she felt safe in his arms. But more than that, she felt comfortable, and it was impossible to deny the attraction she felt for him.

That he was caring for her so tenderly, even after having seen her fully exposed face, was very significant to her, as well. Not only was he a handsome man, but he was also very caring and sweet too.

Rather than take her straight to the front door, he started walking toward the back door of the manor, with Sophia following silently behind them. Despite her lack of surprise, her heart fell. Of course, she was just an employee of his. He would never wish for anyone else in the house to see him helping take care of her.

"It will be best if we go in through the back of the mansion," he whispered, his breath warm and thrilling on her ear. "I cannot bear to subject you to the gawking of the party guests who would see us going through if we went in the front."

Rosalie's heart skipped. He cared nothing for how he looked to anyone, after all. He merely did not want her injury to become the gossip of the *ton*. His continued kindness melted Rosalie's heart, and she found herself wishing he did not have to put her down.

But then another thought occurred to her. What if he was trying to spare himself the humiliation of being spotted with a hideous monster, and he was only sparing her feelings because she was merely his governess?

They entered the house through the back door, but instantly they realized that the duke's plan had failed. Many of the guests had already arrived, and they had spilled all the way down the hallway.

Several of them saw the trio, and Rosalie looked away. But though she could only see people from the edges of her vision, she could feel their eyes on them. She flushed, struggling against the urge to bury her face in the duke's neck. That would be far too scandalous, and she could not bear bringing more shame upon him than she already was.

Through the crowd, the duchess hurried forward and approached them. Rosalie hid her face with one hand, unable to bear the look of horror she was sure the duchess wore. But she felt nothing but surprise when Lady Livinwood spoke.

"My heavens, Miss Stewart, are you all right?" she asked, her voice wrought with worry and concern.

Rosalie uncovered her face, which was now crimson, and nodded weakly.

"It is just my foot," she said, trying to reassure the duchess.

Lady Livinwood gasped.

"Just?" she asked. "My dear, we shall have you tended to at once."

The duke nodded curtly to his mother.

"Edgar has given word for the physician to be sent for," he said. "You go and see the guests, Mother. Everything is under control."

The duchess bit her lip and looked Rosalie over. Rosalie's heart swelled at the woman's kind concern for her wellbeing. She gave her a grateful smile, which the duchess returned with one of great sympathy.

"Very well," she said at last. "Take her to the parlor, darling. I will instruct the butler to escort the physician there when he arrives."

Both the duke and Rosalie nodded, then the duke did as his mother asked and carried her to the parlor.

Chapter Seventeen

Cedric kept his eyes forward as he carried the governess through the manor. He was aware that the party of guests were looking at him, some with curiosity, and others with disdain and distaste. However, they were the least of his concern.

He could not guess how hurt Miss Stewart was, but she appeared to have taken quite a tumble. She had been unconscious when he found her, on top of whatever damage her ankle had suffered. She was his priority. The party guests could just keep whispering and guessing for the time being.

His mother kept the guests mollified while Cedric took Miss Stewart to the parlor. The butler approached, with Sophia's nursemaid following behind, but Sophia made a grand display of ignoring the young woman. He walked over to the sofa, placing Miss Stewart down on it gently. Sophia promptly rushed over to her governess.

"Darling, why don't you go with Miss Jennings?" he asked, gesturing to where the nursemaid stood, looking irritated and inconvenienced.

Sophia shook her head, looking at her father with tear-filled eyes. She did not speak, but Cedric could see she was deeply concerned about her governess. Cedric glanced at the young woman, and their eyes met. The hurt in hers tore at his heart, and he had to look away. But when she cleared her throat, he looked at her once more with the utmost attentiveness.

"You needn't sit with me, your lordship," she said, giving him a half smile. "I know there is a party, and you should attend to your guests so it can begin."

Cedric took a breath. He was well aware the governess was right. She was a mere employee, after all, not a guest or a member of the family. But as he watched her struggle to keep her brave face despite her quite evident pain, he could not help feeling mysteriously compelled to stay with her. He was in quite an odd position, and he was not sure how to handle it.

"Milord," the butler said, his interruption filling Cedric with relief. "Dr. Brock has just arrived."

Cedric turned to face the butler, surveying the elderly man standing beside him.

"Thank you," he said, waving a hand at the butler. "Please, return to assisting my mother."

The butler vanished quickly, and Cedric beckoned the physician inside the room. He approached promptly, quietly exchanging introductions with the governess. Cedric winced, as he should have made such introductions. But his mind was racing, as was his heart. Why was Miss Stewart's injury having such a strange effect on him?

"Your Grace," the physician said, looking at Cedric with kind but firm eyes. "I would ask for privacy so that I may examine Miss Stewart."

Cedric's mind screamed at the doctor that he would not be moved. But propriety held him back. Instead of responding to the physician, he simply nodded. Then, he turned to Sophia, kneeling down to her level.

"Come, dear," he said, taking her hand and standing once more. "Let us allow the doctor to look at Miss Stewart."

His daughter, having no reservations like his own, pulled away from her father and shook her head.

"No," she said sharply. "I shall not leave her. She needs us, Papa."

Cedric's heart ached. He had never before had to tell his daughter no about something she wanted. Her wants had never been those of the spoiled children of the *ton*, and he was always delighted to see her bright smiles and deep gratitude whenever he catered to her wishes. But this time, he had no choice, and it made his soul weep.

"Sophia, my darling," he said, kneeling down to eye level. "We must allow the doctor to help Miss Stewart so that she can get better. I promise you that as soon as he is finished with his examination, you can come back and sit with her."

Sophia's lip trembled, clearly wanting to continue arguing. But then, she looked from the physician, who nodded in gentle agreement, to the governess, who nodded with a reassuring smile. Eventually, Sophia wiped her face with the sleeve of her dress and nodded.

"Fine," she said. "But I shall wait right outside that door. And I will not move."

Cedric smiled despite his wounded heart.

"I would not dream of forcing you to move," he said.

He took his daughter's hand and led her out of the room. They did just as Sophia said, standing just at the edge of the doorway. Though he could hear the guests talking amongst themselves, the party was all but forgotten for Cedric. He prayed the governess's injury was not a severe one. Seeing her so frail and hurt weighed heavily on him.

Quiet sobbing drew his attention back to his daughter. He looked down at her to see she had covered her mouth with her free hand.

Gently, he scooped up the little girl and sat with her in a nearby chair, putting her softly on his lap.

"Sweetheart, don't cry," he said. "I know you are concerned about Miss Stewart. But it is only a hurt foot. I am sure t she will be well again in a matter of days."

Sophia shook her head, her sobs increasing rather than quieting.

"But what if it is broken?" she asked. "And besides that, she is in terrible pain, no matter what is wrong with her, and I do not like it. And what if she had been hurt much worse? What if she hadn't woken up?"

The child covered her face with her hands, continuing to cry. Cedric held his daughter, astounded. If it wasn't clear enough before, it was at that moment: The bond between the governess and his daughter was strong. Stranger still, he was beginning to feel a bond forming with Miss Stewart, as well. Surely, it was only because of his daughter's attachment to the young woman. Wasn't it?

The doctor came out of the room just then, and Sophia leapt from her father's lap, running up to him.

"Is she all right?" she asked, wiping at her tear-streaked face with both her hands. "Please, tell me she's going to be all right."

The physician chuckled, patting Sophia on the head gently and looking at Cedric.

"Miss Stewart will be fine," he said. "Her foot is a bit swollen, and there is a slight sprain. But she was fortunate enough to have not broken or fractured anything. With a few days of rest, she will be as good as new."

Sophia sobbed with relief, clasping her hands together before covering her face again. Cedric was surprised at how much relief he felt, as well. He cleared his throat and shook the physician's hand vigorously.

"Thank you, doctor," he said. "Please, bill me for your services and I shall settle it straightaway. Have a wonderful day, sir."

The physician nodded.

"And a good day to you, Your Grace," he said, dipping his head, and taking his leave.

Sophia grabbed her father's hand and began tugging him toward the parlor.

"Papa, let us see about Miss Stewart now, please?" she begged, pulling him with all her strength.

Cedric's heart squeezed once more, and he allowed his daughter to lead him into the room without protest. The governess looked exhausted but relieved, which in turn brought Cedric relief. It gave Cedric enough comfort to smile at the young woman as his daughter raced up to her.

"How are you feeling, Miss Stewart?" he asked gently, sitting in a chair just beside the governess's head.

"Tired," he said, giving him a small smile. "But thankfully, the doctor does not believe anything is broken. That means that I shall not miss any days of work."

Cedric looked at the young woman as though she were mad.

"You absolutely will," he said with soft admonishment. "In fact, I insist you take the next few days off to rest."

Miss Steward blushed, and Cedric thought she might try to protest. But Sophia gently scooted herself onto the sofa just at her governess's waist and put a small hand on the young woman's cheek.

"I insist, as well, Miss Stewart," she said, pleading. "We cannot enjoy our walks in the garden if you are hurt. And you will only be injured longer if you try to work when you should be resting."

Cedric beamed proudly at his daughter. He had always known she was smart, but she seemed to be positively blossoming under Miss Stewart's tutelage.

The governess seemed impressed, as well. She patted the child on her head and gazed at her fondly.

"Very well, Nurse Sophia," she said, giving Cedric an impish glance. "I suppose I cannot argue with that logic."

Cedric nodded solemnly, suppressing the twitch of a smile at the corners of his mouth.

"Nor can I," he said. "And to that end, I shall arrange for Miss Jennings to look after our little nurse here while you are recovering."

Sophia's face instantly collapsed into a frown. She shook her head firmly and clung to Miss Stewart.

"I don't want Miss Jennings," she said. "I want Miss Stewart."

Cedric bit his lip. The physician had said that rest was important for the governess, and he concurred. But it was clear that Sophia adored her governess, and that the adoration was reciprocated.

"You must listen to your father, darling," Miss Stewart said, smiling sadly at his daughter. "I will miss you, but I am certain that Miss Jennings will allow you to come and visit me once a day until I am well again."

Sophia shook her head, setting her jaw in a way that was clearly meant to be disobedient, but only succeeded in being precious.

"That simply will not do," she said. "I want to keep you company, not let Miss Jennings look after me. I would miss you too much."

The governess opened her mouth to say something further, then she closed it again, looking at Cedric. He already knew he would give into his daughter's request, as it was far from unreasonable. She had said to herself that she would miss his daughter's company while she recovered. And he did not want to discourage Sophia's desire to be loving and caring toward someone.

With a defeated, but loving, sigh, Cedric shrugged his shoulders.

"Very well," he said. "So long as Miss Stewart is feeling up to the company, you may spend your time with her while she recovers."

Sophia ran over to her father, giving him a tight embrace.

"Thank you, Papa," she said. "I promise I will take good care of her."

Cedric looked at Miss Stewart, who was gazing at his daughter fondly.

"I know you will, darling," he said. "But please, do not forget your bedtime."

Sophia frowned again.

"Can't I spend the night in Miss Stewart's room?" she asked. "I will sleep in the chair, and I will not bother her. I promise."

Cedric sighed. He did not wish to have to tell Sophia no, but it was certainly unorthodox to allow her to sleep in the servant's quarters, even if it was with her governess. He chewed his lip, glancing at the governess as he tried to decide what to say.

Chapter Eighteen

"Sophia, dear," Rosalie said to the young girl. "You should listen to your father and do as he tells you. It is not becoming of a young lady to argue with her father."

She meant the words she spoke to the child, and she knew it was what the duke likely expected of his daughter. But Rosalie could not help smiling at Sophia's desire to keep her company.

Never before had she bonded with a child, let alone had a child who fought to spend time with her rather than avoid her. It warmed her heart, and she realized she already loved Sophia dearly.

Sophia moved around her father, taking a seat beside Rosalie once again and wrapped her little arms around Rosalie.

"I am glad you are all right," she said, smiling up at her governess. "I just can't help wanting to spend time with you instead of Miss Jennings. I care about you, Miss Stewart, and I will miss our lessons while you are recovering."

Rosalie's heart skipped a beat. She furiously blinked back tears at the child's affection, fumbling for words. She knew she should continue to insist that Sophia did what the duke told her, but even she was beginning to hope that the duke would change his mind and let the child stay with her each day until she returned to work.

She looked at the duke, only to find him looking at her and Sophia with an expression of awe and wonder. It seemed as though he, too, was moved by Sophia's attachment to Rosalie. And when he looked directly at her, his eyes were intense and warm, which sent tingles down her spine. She held her breath, waiting to see what he would say.

"Cedric," said a sharp, bitter voice from the doorway.

Rosalie knew to whom the voice belonged before she looked up. Lady Olivia stood scowling at her brother, her arms folded across her chest. *No*, Rosalie realized, her stomach twisting into knots, *she is scowling at me.*

Cedric gave Rosalie a sheepish look before turning to face his sister.

"Yes?" he asked.

Olivia lifted her chin, narrowing her eyes until they were naught but slits.

"Some of the guests are asking after you," she said, her voice dripping with poison. "Lady Isabel, in particular, is concerned about your whereabouts."

The knot in Rosalie's stomach tightened as the duke slowly rose from his seat beside her. Only then did she realize she did not want him to leave her. But as he gave her an apologetic smile, she did her best to look brave and unfazed.

"Tell the guests I will be with them shortly, please," he said.

"But Brother—" Lady Olivia began.

Cedric held up a hand, glancing at his sister pointedly.

"I shall join the party shortly," he said. "I must see Miss Stewart safely to her room first."

Lady Olivia stood there a moment longer. Her eyes were filled with malice and fury, and she glowered at Rosalie. Rosalie swallowed, terribly uncomfortable. She prayed the young woman would heed her brother and take her leave.

When she finally obeyed the duke's command, Rosalie could not help exhaling a heavy sigh of relief. The duke, seeming to mistake it for a gasp of pain, leapt straight to her side.

"Do you need assistance getting to your bedchambers?" he asked, reaching toward her as though he had already decided he must help her.

Rosalie bit her lip. The pain was still terrible, but she knew she should forgo any further help from the duke. She had already put him in a position of embarrassment in front of a whole drove of party guests. And Lady Olivia's glowering had made it quite clear that Rosalie was nothing more than a mere servant. The least she could do was maintain some of her dignity and get herself to her room alone.

"I will manage, your lordship," she said, mustering a smile. "Thank you kindly for all of your help, but I really must not keep you from your party any longer."

The duke, surprisingly, looked as though he wished to insist on staying to help her. To emphasize her determination to get herself to her room, she stood, albeit slowly, giving him another smile. Reluctantly, the duke bowed, returning Rosalie's small smile with a weak one of his own.

"You are a strong woman, Miss Stewart," he said. "I commend you for that, to be sure. I shall take my leave. But be sure to send word to me if you need anything."

Rosalie nodded.

"Forgive me for not curtseying as I should," she said, holding out the sides of her dress and smiling. "But perhaps, just this once, we can just imagine it."

The duke laughed and shook his head.

"I would never dream of expecting you to curtsey with an injured foot," he said. "But the respect and sentiment are appreciated. Good evening, Miss Stewart."

Rosalie dipped her head.

"Good evening, Your Grace," she said.

As her father walked away, Sophia reached up and took Rosalie's hand. She smiled up at her, putting her free hand on the small of Rosalie's back.

"I will help you to your room, Miss Stewart," she said. "I am strong, and I know I can do it."

Rosalie looked down at the child, her heart warm despite the pain, and Lady Olivia's icy glares.

"You mustn't worry yourself about me, Sophia," she said. "I am sure I can get to my room on my own, as long as I move slowly and with great care."

Sophia looked at her with wide, pleading eyes.

"I still feel I'm to blame for what happened," she said. "Please, let me help you, if only this little bit."

Rosalie thought for a moment. She could not fathom allowing the child of a duke to support her while she hobbled along. But what was the harm in letting Sophia feel as though she was helping?

"Very well," she said. "You may continue to hold my hand and walk with me up the stairs. It would be a good idea to have someone with me, anyway."

Sophia brightened for the first time since Rosalie's accident, and she nodded in fervent agreement.

"I would be positively delighted," she said.

Slowly, Rosalie and Sophia made their way out of the parlor and up the stairs. It was not long before Rosalie regretted her decision to walk on her injured foot and, by the time they reached her bedchambers, she could barely walk at all. But she forced herself to keep the pain out of her expression, breathing a silent sigh of relief as she settled onto her bed.

"Are you all right?" Sophia asked, standing back while Rosalie made herself as comfortable as possible on her bed.

Rosalie nodded, doing her best to hide the grimace of pain as she tried to put her foot on one of her pillows.

"I am fine," she lied. "You may go to your own room, if you like."

Sophia shook her head.

"I wish to stay with you until you fall asleep," she insisted. "I will even sit in the chair beside your bed instead of on the bed with you, so I won't hurt you. Please, Miss Stewart?"

Rosalie bit her lip. She knew it was getting late and that the duke would expect his daughter to be in bed soon. And she did not wish to interact with Irene, should she come in search of the girl to put her to bed. But she struggled to make herself hold firm to tell the child to leave.

"Now, Miss Sophia," said a voice from the door, which was swinging open just as the person on the other side knocked. "Your bedtime is in just one hour, and you must not disobey your father."

Rosalie smiled as Beth entered the room. She walked over to Sophia and patted her on the head, and then she went over to Rosalie's bedside.

"I am glad to see you, Beth," Rosalie said truthfully.

Beth nodded, fussing over Rosalie's blankets and fluffing her pillows.

"I should imagine you are," she said. "You must be starved." She turned back to Sophia. "And you really must go to Irene and get yourself ready for bed, my dear."

Sophia stuck out her bottom lip, looking at Rosalie with her beautiful, wide eyes.

"Please, can I stay with Miss Stewart until she falls asleep?" she asked.

Beth shook her head, kneeling before her to place soft hands on the girl's arms.

"Your father would not like that at all," she said. "You would not want Miss Stewart to get into trouble now, would you?"

Sophia shrugged.

"He never did say whether I could spend the night here with Miss Stewart," she said. "Therefore, he could not be angry at me if I were to do so."

Both Beth and Rosalie laughed.

"What she says is true," Rosalie said to Beth in confirmation. "However, my darling, I believe he is likely trusting us to abide by his wishes. We mustn't abuse his generosity, as he has already granted you permission to spend lots of time with me during the day. We oughtn't to give him a reason to regret that, ought we?"

Sophia shook her head, looked back at Rosalie, then to Beth once more, and sighed heavily.

"Very well," she said with obvious reluctance. "But may I please come back in here first thing in the morning?"

Rosalie beckoned the child over to her, embracing her. She raised her eyebrows inquisitively at Beth, who nodded with a sly smile.

"Of course, you may, darling," she said.

Beth held out her hand to Sophia, giving her a kind smile.

"Now, let us get you to your room, so I can go and fetch Miss Stewart some dinner," she said.

Sophia nodded. After a reluctant farewell, she allowed Beth to lead her from the room.

Alone for the moment, Rosalie exhaled deeply, resting her head against the wall behind the bed. It had been a trying day, both physically and emotionally, and yet her mind raced. She had been mortified about falling into that rabbit hole, and yet everyone had been so kind and concerned. One person, in particular.

Despite what his nasty sister had said to her, Rosalie could not deny that the duke had seemed genuinely concerned about her. Had he not, he would have sent servants to tend to her. He certainly would not have personally carried her inside the mansion. She smiled to herself and shivered as she recalled the way it had felt, being in his strong arms. Inappropriate or not, that was something she knew she would never forget.

She was glad when Beth returned with her dinner tray. She was, indeed, hungry, and she needed to pull herself from her thoughts of the duke.

"Thank you, Beth," Rosalie said as the housekeeper put the tray beside her bed.

Beth nodded, squeezing Rosalie's arm gently.

"How are you feeling?" she asked.

Rosalie patted her leg softly.

"The pain is starting to subside," she said. "Truthfully, knowing that it isn't broken, I wish I could just get back to work."

Beth shook her head defiantly.

"I am glad you are feeling better," she said. "However, the duchess had given me strict instructions to personally see to it that you rest."

Rosalie blushed. She was unaccustomed to such kind and considerate treatment, especially from her employers. Lord and Lady Winsdale had been kind, but they would have never made such a fuss over her if she had been sick or injured.

"The Livinwood's are truly wonderful people," she said, thinking of the duke's warm smile as she spoke.

Beth, clueless to her thoughts, merely nodded in agreement.

"They are, indeed," she said. "My apologies, dear, but I must return to my duties. Do not hesitate to call me if you need something, however. I shall come to check in with you before I retire for the evening, as well."

Rosalie smiled at her.

"Thank you again," she said. "I will repay your kindness."

Beth shrugged.

"It is my pleasure, Rosalie," she said. "You can repay my kindness by eating your dinner."

Rosalie giggled.

"You need not fret," she said. "I am ravenous."

Beth nodded, patting her hand.

"Good," she said. "I shall take my leave, but I am just a call away."

With that, she left the room, leaving Rosalie alone once more. Rosalie took the tray of food and began to eat, surprised at how good her appetite was. As she ate, she thought about what Beth had said about the duchess insisting she do nothing but rest, and about the duke.

They were indeed kind people to treat her as if he were part of the family, especially considering her physical blemish. But could she ever be anything more than a mere governess, especially to the duke?

Chapter Nineteen

Olivia stormed away from the parlor in a huff, furious with her brother. *How can he sit there, fawning over an injured servant?* Her face contorted into a mask of disgust. *Especially one as hideous as that woman?*

Her lady's maid, Tess, was waiting for her when she reached her bedchambers. She had hoped to be dressed and ready before the guests were due. But that damnable governess and her injury had upset the entire household, and just as the guests arrived too.

Olivia felt deep shame and embarrassment. How could she face any of the suitors present that evening, knowing they had witnessed such a display? Moreover, how could her own family not be as humiliated as she was?

"Make it quick," she snapped, gesturing to the dress Tess had laid out for her in her absence. "The party will begin any minute." Tess flinched, but she did as her mistress commanded. She quickly helped Olivia change into the fresh, brand-new green dress she had selected, then rushed Olivia over to the vanity to fix her hair.

Olivia sighed with frustration, knowing it would likely take the maid more than half an hour to style her hair. But rather than wasting more time scolding the woman, Olivia simply sat still, stewing over her hatred of the governess.

If it had been one of the other servants, Olivia told herself, she would not have been so upset with her brother. In fact, she herself might have expressed marginal concern for their wellbeing. But it was Miss Stewart, that beast of a woman, and Olivia could never reconcile herself to the thought that such a monstrosity deserved such attention.

Moreover, no one could deny the attraction that clearly existed between her brother and the governess. Olivia had been sure at first that it was just the governess inappropriately flirting with her brother. But she could no longer deny that Cedric felt something for the beastly woman, as well.

Perhaps he was not thinking clearly, Olivia thought, trying to explain away her brother's unsavory behavior. But the thought dissolved as soon as it formed. As he'd carried that woman through the mansion, he was aware of all the guests. And yet, he had doted on her the whole way, as though none of them existed.

They all knew it, too, if the whispers amongst them were any indication. The only favor the turmoil did for her was that no one noticed she was present but still not properly dressed for the party. She sighed and shook her head, causing Tess to tug a bit roughly on her hair. She slapped the maid's hand.

"Gently, if you please," she hissed.

The maid nodded meekly.

"Forgive me," she whispered, going back to her task with fingers as light as a butterfly's landing.

Olivia huffed again, but she sat still. The whole incident would surely lead to scandalous gossip within the *ton*. Perhaps now, though, she could reason with her mother. Her previous protests had failed, but now the entire *ton* had witnessed such a shameful display, maybe the duchess could be convinced to get rid of the ugly woman.

Can I take that chance? She wondered to herself, thinking back to the way her family had reacted when she tried to voice her concerns about the governess before she started working for them. For a reason Olivia could not understand, they seemed ready to defend the woman. She doubted they would ever see that the hideous creature was nothing more than a blight on Society, and on their good name.

The only way she could ensure that her family did not suffer the fate of so many other permanently disgraced people and families within the *ton* was for her to take matters into her own hands. If she could not get her mother and brother to see how damaging that young woman's presence was to them, then she vowed to do everything she could to make the governess quit.

Truthfully, that was the best plan. The whole *ton* surely knew now that the beastly woman was in their employ. But it could be argued that kindness and a sense of duty had made her family hire Miss Stewart.

If the woman quit her job, that would bring pity to her family for having their generosity so carelessly tossed aside. There were plenty more governesses available. It would not be long before they hired another one, one without a blemish, and their reputation would be safe.

She smiled to herself, beginning to feel better now she was forming a plan to rid her family of the plague with which they lived. Whatever gossip would ensue because of her brother's thoughtless coddling of a servant could be explained away with claims of temporary sympathy and a lack of desire to have his daughter be traumatized by witnessing any more of the governess's display than was necessary. By the time Tess was finished with Olivia's hair, she was almost in perfect spirits again.

"You look beautiful, your ladyship," the maid said, giving her mistress a tentative smile.

Olivia gave her a smug grin.

"I do, don't I?" she asked. "That is all, Tess. You are dismissed."

The maid's face fell, and she skittered out of the room. Olivia turned to admire herself in the mirror once more before also leaving her bedchambers. As she reached the staircase, she could hear guests' voices drifting from the direction of the drawing room. She was relieved, knowing she had not missed the call for dinner. Perhaps the evening could be salvaged yet.

She had just reached the bottom of the staircase when she heard familiar voices. She looked up to see Lady Isabel and Lord Burtondale heading to the drawing room, as well. When the viscount's eyes met hers, he gave her a slow, warm smile that sent butterflies mad in her stomach. It was all she could do to maintain her composure and curtsey to the viscount and his sister without swooning.

"Good evening, Lady Olivia," the viscount said. He bowed to her, taking her gloved hand and kissing it softly as he righted himself.

"Good evening, Viscount Burtondale," she replied, briefly forgetting his sister was standing beside him. In that moment, Olivia forgot everything apart from the way that the viscount was smiling at her. "Are you enjoying yourself?"

"The party is yet to start, Sister," Cedric's voice echoed throughout the foyer of the mansion. "But I speak confidently when I say that Edgar and Isabel will absolutely enjoy themselves."

Olivia spared her brother a glance, noticing he was approaching, their mother on his arm. But she was nonplussed by the interruption, as the viscount was still smiling sweetly at her.

"I dare say I shall not be disappointed in the evening," he agreed, staring into her eyes. She fought to suppress the shivers that raced up and down her spine as the duchess exchanged greetings with Isabel and Cedric patted his friend on the back.

"Sister, you look absolutely radiant," her brother said, giving her a fond smile.

Olivia returned it, giving her brother a small curtsey.

"Thank you," she said.

For just a moment, it was easy to forget about the debacle with the heinous governess. Especially when the viscount nodded in agreement with the duke's words. Olivia felt herself blush, and she forced herself to look away from him. It would not do for her mother or brother to catch her looking at the viscount in such a scandalous way.

Not that she much minded, as it would likely result in the two of them spending much of the evening together. And that, she well knew, could lead to a courtship with Lord Burtondale.

"You both look lovely," the duchess said, kissing both younger women on the cheek. "And you look dashing, Viscount Burtondale. I am so glad I caught you before the party becomes hectic. I want to personally thank you for being so gracious in helping us with our dear governess."

Olivia's heart sank instantly. Her cheeks flushed more deeply still, this time out of shame rather than excitement. She looked down at the ground, unable to meet the viscount's eyes to see his reaction.

"It was my pleasure, Lady Livinwood," he said, bowing to the duchess. "I do hope she will recover fully."

Olivia squirmed. She knew he must be as repulsed by that woman as the rest of *the* ton. It spoke volumes to her that he would show such kindness to such an ugly creature, but she felt sure he had only done it as a favor to her family. What did he secretly think about the governess? Would his reputation be damaged for having been put in a position of having to help her as he had? Would he blame her if it was?

"Should we..." Olivia began, but Lady Isabel had already begun speaking.

"That was an unfortunate incident," she said. "I wish her a speedy recovery."

Olivia clenched her teeth together and shifted her weight impatiently. She struggled with herself to keep from huffing aloud and exhibiting her irritation. That would have been unseemly and unladylike, and with the viscount standing beside her, she would not allow herself to do it.

"I have ensured she gets plenty of rest," her mother said. "The physician said that it was not broken, fortunately. In a few days, she should be just fine."

The viscount looked relieved. Olivia was agitated that he seemed so concerned with the welfare of a lowly, hideous employee. However, it did speak to the kindness of his heart. Still, Olivia wanted him focused on her, not Miss Stewart.

"That is wonderful, indeed," he said.

Olivia sighed. It annoyed her greatly that they were still discussing that horrifying woman and her foolish escapade earlier. She had no doubt that the woman had injured herself on purpose in an effort to gain the attention of Cedric.

She shuddered at the thought. It would be humiliating enough if her brother ever took a liking to any servant. But it was laughable to think he could care for one as ugly as Rosalie Stewart.

When the butler approached, Olivia felt sure she had never been gladder to see one of the servants. She cleared her throat as a gesture for the butler to speak. He looked at her with a furrowed brow, no doubt expecting her brother to be the one to acknowledge him, but he bowed and smiled.

"Dinner is ready to be served," he said.

Cedric bowed to him.

"Thank you," he said. "You may tell the rest of the guests, if you have not done so already."

The butler excused himself, while Cedric turned back to their small group.

"Shall we?" he asked, holding out his arm out to their mother. To Olivia's surprise, the viscount offered one of his arms to her too.

"Of course, milord," he said in response to Cedric's question, but he was looking straight at her.

"Indeed, we shall," she said, her cheeks flushing as she slipped her hand into his arm.

Chapter Twenty

Cedric gave Lady Isabel a polite smile as she made some remark he barely heard. He was partnered with her as her escort into the dining room, and he had to admit to himself that she was very beautiful.

It was hard to recall the way she had been when he last saw her all those years ago. She was also very poised and witty, and he did not find her company entirely unpleasant. So, why did he still feel as though she was merely an acquaintance?

An image of Miss Stewart came to his mind. Her face sent tingles down his spine and seeing her in so much pain tugged at his heart in a way he had never experienced before. And she was so good and kind to Sophia, which in itself was unusual. But so often he found he simply could not stop thinking about her beautiful, jade-green eyes.

She is my daughter's governess, for heaven's sake, he thought, mentally shaking himself. *What is it about her that could possibly be making me feel this way?*

"Your Grace?" Lady Isabel said, disrupting his internal chastising. "Are you all right?"

Cedric felt himself blush as he looked down at her and smiled. He knew he needed to snap himself out of it. It was no use entertaining such thoughts, least of all when he was supposed to be entertaining guests.

"Yes, Lady Isabel," he said, doing his best to sound casual and convincing. "I am fine."

He offered nothing more in the way of an explanation, only continuing to smile at the young woman beside him. She seemed satisfied, though, as she resumed telling him some story that he sheepishly realized he had missed half of. But fortunately, they then reached the dining hall, and he was able to put his attention on escorting Lady Isabel to her seat, just to the right of the head of the table, and then making his way to his own.

As the rest of the guests found their seats, Cedric prepared himself. He was expected to make a welcoming toast, but his thoughts were still in disarray. He pretended to be very interested in the servant pouring him a glass of wine.

While the other guests were busy waiting for their own wine, he practiced his smile. But in the back of his mind, thoughts of the governess still lingered. He made a promise to himself to check in on her as soon as the party ended. With that, he began to relax, at least enough to address his mother and his guests.

"May I have your attention?" he asked, raising his glass as the last of the guests were served their wine. "Before we begin the meal, I would just like to thank all of you for coming this evening. It is my sincere hope you all enjoy yourselves tonight. And if you find that you are not enjoying yourselves at any time, please feel free to help yourselves to more wine."

The guests laughed heartily at his jest, making Cedric smile. The evening was off to a good start, and he thought he might not hate the party as much as he had feared, after all.

"That was a lovely toast," Lady Isabel said, smiling sweetly at Cedric as he took his seat.

He nodded politely to her.

"That is very kind of you," he said. "I only thought of it as I stood up to address everyone."

The young woman put a hand on her chest, looking quite impressed.

"I am sure I could never do such a thing," she said, her voice filled with genuine appreciation. "I can address people when I must, but I cannot do so without thinking over what I will say for some time beforehand."

Cedric shrugged, giving her a genuine smile.

"It comes with practice, I suppose," he said. "And it helps if you get comfortable with making a fool of yourself, because it happens often, in my experience."

Lady Isabel laughed, a real, true laugh. Cedric realized she was easy to talk to; she was not fake or putting on a show to impress him, and she was not a snob or a featherbrain, like many of the other women of the *ton* he had encountered. He found himself laughing with her, simply because he was enjoying her company.

"You are as funny as you are heroic," she said, suddenly becoming more serious. "That was a very noble thing you did earlier, helping your injured governess."

Cedric flushed, bracing himself for ridicule. If Lady Isabel was putting on an act to attract him to her, he would soon see it. But instead, she simply smiled fondly at him, waiting patiently for him to respond.

"I simply did what needed to be done," he said, suddenly feeling shy.

Lady Isabel leaned forward, giving him a look of awe.

"You showed how kind and compassionate your heart is," she said. "Few gentlemen would have done what you did. You know as well as I do, they would have simply sent servants to tend to an employee. Your actions are both commendable and admirable, and I believe you should be proud."

Cedric had to will his mouth to not fall open. She was as humble as she was pretty, and she demonstrated not only empathy, but also a strong ability to support people she cared for. Cedric hated to admit it, even secretly, but Lady Isabel would make a fine wife.

"May I have your attention?" his mother said, causing Cedric to jump as she took her turn addressing the guests. "I trust that dinner was to your liking. With the conclusion of the meal, the dance floor is now opening. Please, make your way to the ballroom at your leisure."

Cedric blushed, looking at his half-eaten plate of food. He had been so involved in his conversation with Lady Isabel that he had not noted the passing of time during the meal. With a sheepish grin, he rose, offering his arm to Lady Isabel.

"Shall we?" he asked.

Lady Isabel nodded, her eyes wide with excitement.

"We shall," she said, taking his arm.

Cedric was impressed by the vibrant décor his mother had arranged in the ballroom. He knew she had been making plans since before they left London, but he was still impressed to see how she had made everything appear so beautiful in such a short time.

There were gold candlesticks and candelabras on every flat surface, and the chandeliers sparkled with a fresh, clean shine, and glowed with brand-new white candles.

There were purple and red flowers in crystal vases, and purple and red banners all throughout the room. His mother had ensured there were four long refreshment tables, filled end-to-end with pastries, iced treats, and bowls of mint punch, as well as flutes of champagne and glasses of wine. She had done a lovely job, indeed, and he was proud. He also held out hope that his sister would be successful in finding suitors that night. Nothing would make him happier than to host callers for her over the coming days and weeks.

"May I see your dance card?" Cedric asked as he gently released Lady Isabel's arm.

The young woman blushed again and smiled brightly, handing him the card.

"You certainly may, Your Grace," she said.

Cedric scanned the card, securing a dance for later in the evening. He watched as his friend's sister radiated her excitement, and he could not help smiling in return. She really was a lovely young woman and he did not mind spending more time with her. Though she was far from the main thing on his mind.

He handed her back her card, bidding her a warm good evening. Then, he took his leave, trying not to appear overly eager as he made his way to the refreshment table. He took a glass of wine, drinking from it heartily.

The party was hardly as unpleasant as some affairs he'd attended within the *ton*, largely due to it being hosted in his own home, where he felt comfortable. But he would be untruthful if he said he wasn't looking forward to the end of the evening.

He saw his mother approaching, and he took up a flute of champagne, handing it to her when she reached him.

"You have done a marvelous job, Mother," he said, kissing her cheek.

The duchess toasted her son, sharing a drink with him before replying.

"I feel there may be much to celebrate this evening," she said, her eyes sparkling. "I could not help noticing that you marked a dance on Isabel's dance card."

Cedric rolled his eyes playfully, chuckling to himself.

"Do you have eyes in all the banners in the room?" he asked.

The duchess shook her head.

"No, I was just behind you as you escorted her in here," she said. "I overheard you just as I was moving to greet some late arriving guests."

Cedric nodded.

"She is a very lovely young woman," he said. "And it seemed only right to ask her to dance."

His mother nodded, looking at him with pleased scrutiny.

"Well, I hope you have a wonderful evening, darling," she said. "Now, if you will excuse me, I must do some more mingling."

Cedric laughed, kissing his mother as he bade her a good evening and watched her disappear into the crowd. He drank his wine, content to stand and let his thoughts wander.

"The bottom of that glass is dangerously close to being visible, my friend," Edgar said.

His friend startled him, and he nearly choked on the remainder of his wine. He cleared his throat, narrowing his eyes at the viscount.

"Had I ended up wearing that, you would have worn two glasses," he said, playfully nudging Edgar's shoulder with the heel of his hand.

Edgar laughed.

"I am sure there are far worse things to wear than wine, Cedric," he said.

"Try me," Cedric teased. "Tell me, what brings you over here to disrupt my peace and quiet?"

Edgar suddenly became more serious than Cedric had ever seen him.

"Cedric," he said slowly. "You know I am not much for gossip. Especially when it comes from certain snobs. However, I have heard some terrible rumors about your governess."

Cedric's heart stopped. He set aside his empty glass and faced his friend squarely.

"What rumors?" he said, trying to keep the defensiveness out of his voice.

Edgar leaned forward, keeping his voice hushed.

"People are saying that she has a beastly appearance," he said.

Cedric stared at Edgar, his stomach twisting into knots. The young woman's face had been exposed after she fell. Had his friend not seen the birthmark on her cheek? Or could it be that he had seen it, but he did not see it as beastly, as some other people apparently did?

"You cannot believe the gossips," he said sharply, suddenly feeling very protective of Miss Stewart.

Cedric's tone change surprised Edgar. His eyes widened, and he opened his mouth to speak. But just then, the orchestra struck the chords of the next dance set. Cedric remembered his dance with Lady Isabel, and he bowed stiffly to his friend.

"Forgive me, Edgar," he said, smiling tightly. "I must go and claim a dance I requested earlier this evening."

He turned and left Edgar slack-jawed, no doubt curious about Cedric's strange behavior. But he would have to speak privately with his friend later. He put on his best smile as he approached Lady Isabel, bringing back all his earlier charm as he led her onto the dance floor.

But as they danced, he could think of nothing but Miss Stewart. He tried to tell himself he was offended by the rumors about her because of his own little Sophia's affliction. He knew well, after all, how cruel people could be to someone because of an abnormality in their appearance, without bothering to get to know them.

However, as he thought about the injustice, his heart broke for the governess. She was every bit as sweet and kind as his daughter, and very wise. And, he believed, she was easily the most beautiful woman in London, birthmark or not. It would not have mattered if the mark had covered her entire face. She was still lovelier, both inside and out, than the rest of the *ton* put together.

You have feelings for her, said a voice in his head. The voice was not his own, however. It was the voice of his father. *No use in denying it, my boy. You feel a very strong attraction and affection for her.* And, without a doubt, Cedric knew it was true.

Chapter Twenty-one

For the next two days, Sophia visited Rosalie several times a day. And both nights, Sophia slipped back into Rosalie's room after she was supposed to be tucked in for bed to read books to her. Rosalie would not dream of telling the duke about his daughter's disobedience.

However, if he ever found out, Rosalie would firmly tell him that she had asked Sophia to practice reading while she was unable to give lessons. She knew it could likely get her into trouble, but she did not mind. She adored Sophia, and she could not stand the thought of the sweet girl getting into trouble, especially not just for being so kind to her.

On the third day, Rosalie found she experienced almost no pain when she rose from her bed. It was early yet, almost an hour before Sophia was due to come and visit her. She paced around her bedchambers a few times, testing to be sure her ankle would no longer trouble her. With each lap she made around the room, her level of pain only improved, so she dressed quickly. If she hurried, she could surprise Sophia by starting lessons again that very day.

Rosalie slipped quietly down the hall. If the duke or duchess saw her, she wanted it to be while she was already in the midst of giving the day's lessons. She knew they would not be angry with her, but she did not want them trying to make her rest any longer.

She dearly missed teaching Sophia, and she was anxious to once again be useful to Livinwood. Besides, she was going crazy being stuck in her room. Truthfully, she likely would have returned to work, even if the pain was still great.

She reached the door to Sophia's bedchambers just as Irene stepped out. Rosalie held her breath as the young woman glared at her. Irene looked her over, her lip curling up in bitter disdain.

Without a word, she turned on her heel and walked away. Rosalie sighed with relief, collecting herself for a brief moment before stepping into the child's room.

Princess was first to greet Rosalie. The puppy scampered over to her, standing on her hind legs, and pawing at Rosalie's dress. Sophia noticed right away, gasping as she ran to her governess.

"Princess," Sophia scolded firmly, scooping up the animal in her arms. "Do not be a bad dog." Then, she looked up at Rosalie wearing both a thrilled and confused expression. "What are you doing in here, Miss Stewart? Are you not supposed to be convalescing?"

Rosalie clapped her hands for the young girl, smiling at her with pride.

"I am happy to see you have been practicing your vocabulary," she said. "Do not be so hard on Princess, though. She is only showing her affection the only way she knows how." She stroked the puppy's head as she spoke, then looked at Sophia again. "I came to ask if you are ready to begin your lessons again today."

Sophia's whole face lit up, and she clasped her hands together and positioned them beneath her chin.

"I am positively bursting," she said. "I have dearly missed our lessons, Miss Stewart. I have especially missed spending time outside together."

Rosalie's lip trembled as the girl echoed her own earlier thoughts. She loved the girl more with every minute she spent with her, and she was so grateful for the bond she had forged with her.

"I have missed our time outside, as well," Rosalie said, adopting her governess's voice. "However, you know the rule. We must get through our lessons first."

Sophia nodded, setting her jaw with concentration and determination.

"Then, let us begin," she said.

Rosalie chose penmanship as the first lesson for the day. She wrote first individual letters, and then full words, on the blackboard, and asked Sophia to copy them. In just an hour, Sophia had already mastered half of the alphabet, and she had made significant progress on the remaining letters.

She worked hard, and by the end of the lesson, she held up a piece of paper with one small sentence written on it:

I love Princess.

Rosalie applauded Sophia, taking the paper from her gently and putting it in the chalk tray, so it was displayed proudly against the blackboard.

"Marvelous job, Sophia," she said, beaming at the child. "Now, make ready. Our next lesson will be conducted in the music room."

Sophia gasped.

"Truly?" she asked, grinning.

Rosalie nodded eagerly.

"Truly," she said. "I will give you a basic lesson in pianoforte."

Sophia clapped, stooping down to pick up Princess and twirl around in a circle with her.

"Do you hear that, Princess?" she asked. "I shall be a grand pianoforte player soon."

Rosalie laughed, ushering the enthusiastic child out of the room and down the stairs. She had no idea of Sophia's musical skills but, if her other lessons were any indication, she would, indeed, have an impressive grasp of the instrument in just a few lessons.

Moments later, Rosalie and Sophia were seated, side by side, at the pianoforte. The Livinwood music room was grander than any she had ever seen. The music selection was vast, as well, and it did not take Rosalie long to find a piece sufficiently simple for a young beginner.

"Let us begin with hand positioning," Rosalie said, poising her hands over the keys. "You must keep your fingers curved, as your touch must be light on the keys."

Sophia mimicked Rosalie's finger curvature and position on the keys. She pressed notes for a minute, giggling at the dissonant music that came forth from the instrument each time.

"That sounds horrible," she admitted. "But it is great fun."

Rosalie nodded, giving her a patient smile.

"The next part of the lesson will help you to sound much better," she said. "Because now that you know how to press the keys, I can start teaching you what they are."

Sophia clapped, watching Rosalie intently.

"As you know, the alphabet begins with the letter A," Rosalie said. "However, the octaves on the pianoforte begin with the C key."

Sophia furrowed her brow.

"So, it goes from C to Z?" she asked.

Rosalie giggled, shaking her head.

"No, darling," she said. "An octave consists of eight keys. There are eight note letters for the pianoforte. So, the octave begins on the C of the first octave and ends on the C of the next octave."

Sophia's eyes lit up.

"Which means that C both begins and ends an octave," she said.

Rosalie nodded, smiling.

"That is correct," she said. "Now, let us practice some scales, so that you can get accustomed to playing the notes by their names."

Sophia nodded, watching carefully as Rosalie pressed each key and gave her the name of the notes. Sophia was delighted when she heard the sharps and flats of the ebony keys, and she shivered when Rosalie played a few chords using only those keys.

"Those sound like church music," she said, giggling.

Rosalie nodded.

"Those are called minor chords," she said. "Many church hymns use those. Many composers use them, as well, in requiem pieces."

Sophia nodded solemnly, though Rosalie could see she was getting restless with all the explanations and anxious to play some on the instrument by herself. Rosalie went back to the ivory keys, showing her first how to play a C chord with her right and left hands separately, and then how to play them together.

"Now," she said, scooting over and removing her hands from the keys. "It is your turn."

Sophia shrieked, quickly composing herself and positioning her hands just the way Rosalie had shown her. Then, she slowly worked her way through the scale, just as Rosalie had taught. On her very first try, she got it right, both with her hands individually, and with them together. She turned to look at her instructor expectantly. Rosalie patted her on the back, grinning.

"Very well done, Sophia," she said, marveling at the child's progress. "I am impressed at how quickly you are learning."

Sophia's proud expression alone could have brightened the room as she practiced the scale again and again. Soon, she could play it nearly as fast as Rosalie could, and with the same level of perfection.

"What is next?" Sophia asked.

Rosalie showed her more basic scales that began with the other major notes. Sophia learned those even more quickly, which left Rosalie in awe. Never had she seen a child learn the pianoforte so quickly, and she vowed she would do everything she could to encourage the girl's progress.

They got through what would have normally taken Rosalie a week's worth of lessons in less than an hour. Sophia looked hungry for more to learn, so Rosalie decided to do something she had never done before with a student during her first lesson.

"Would you like to try reading a little music?" she asked.

Sophia gasped, bouncing up and down on the pianoforte's bench. To Rosalie's surprise, Princess, though panting excitedly and drooling, sat obediently throughout the entire lesson at the little girl's feet.

"I would love that, Miss Stewart," she said.

Chapter Twenty-two

"Cedric," Olivia sang as Cedric tried to tiptoe past the main dining hall. "Lunch has just been served. You will come and join us, won't you?"

Cedric winced, mentally cursing his confounded sister. She'd ensured he had not missed a single one of the house party events since the night of the ball. There had been many, and the entrance and exit of so many guests had been exhausting for him. Also, he had not seen or heard word of the governess since she was injured, and he simply wished to see about her, as he had intended to do after the ball.

He could not help wondering if Olivia was doing it on purpose. She had made her dislike of the governess very well known, after all. But why should she do such a thing? Miss Stewart's presence in their home had virtually no effect on Olivia. If she hated her so much, she could simply stay away from her.

"Of course, Sister dear," he said, backing up and entering the dining room. Everyone had turned to stare after his sister's loud, uncouth announcement, but it was hardly the first they had witnessed since their arrival. He stood up perfectly straight and gave her a wicked grin. "I would never have guessed you cannot stand to be without me."

The guests chuckled, but Olivia's smile faltered briefly.

"I do you a favor by showing these good people my affection for you," she said. "Without that, they would all find you hopeless."

Cedric grinned more widely as he made his way to his seat.

"Or is it that they would learn how hopeless you are without me?" he retorted.

The room filled with another hearty bout of laughter. Olivia blinked sweetly at him, wrinkling her nose.

"You do flatter yourself, Brother," she said, winking at him. But her eyes looked strange and dark, and Cedric wondered why. Before he could ponder too deeply, however, she turned to the person beside her and began chatting animatedly.

With a shrug, Cedric began to partake of the lunch feast of roast duck, striking up a conversation of his own with a gentleman whose name he could not recall. Outwardly, he was ever the polite, gracious host. But inside, all he wanted was to slip away from the endless sea of guests and go and see about his governess and his daughter.

As if answering his unspoken question, he heard music drifting faintly down the hall from the music room. He glanced around, noting that everyone else was busy talking and enjoying their meal.

He quietly excused himself from the gentleman to whom he had been talking, promising to return soon before slipping out, blessedly unnoticed by his difficult sister. He tiptoed down the hall, wondering who could be making such beautiful music, with his mother and sister both in the dining room.

He entered the room, and his heart began to pound in his chest. There sat Miss Stewart, playing a song on the pianoforte that Cedric believed was a piece from Beethoven. It took him a moment to realize that Sophia was sitting right beside her, watching intently, and that the governess was giving his daughter a pianoforte lesson.

He stood, unmoving, enthralled with the music coming from the pianoforte. Something about her playing sent tingles down his spine. The piano was positioned just so the governess and his daughter could not see him. He felt terrible for spying on a lesson, but he was incapable of movement or speech. He thought he had never heard a sound as beautiful as her playing, and it had him under a magic spell.

He was so hypnotized that, when Princess greeted him with a friendly bark, as she always did, Cedric nearly jumped out of his skin. It startled Miss Steward and Sophia, as well, as they both whirled around and looked toward the doorway. Sophia was smiling brightly, but the governess's cheeks flushed a deep crimson. Instantly, Cedric felt awful for eavesdropping on her playing. But he could never bring himself to regret it.

"Forgive me," he said, fumbling for an excuse as to why he was there in the first place. "I thought Sophia had been left unsupervised while you were resting. I did not know you had resumed lessons."

The words sounded fictitious, even to his own ears. But the governess simply shook her head, giving him a sheepish smile.

"I apologize if our music lesson was disruptive to your family or your guests," she said.

Cedric shook his head, but his words caught in his throat. Her jade-green eyes sparkled against her blushing cheeks, and his heart felt like melting butter as he looked at her. She was positively breathtaking. What's more, she was not breaking eye contact. It would be scandalous, indeed, if they were caught. But she was so beautiful that he did not care. Did she, perhaps, feel the same way about him?

"Papa," Sophia said, rushing over to him. "I am going to be just as good as Miss Stewart at playing the pianoforte."

Cedric lifted his daughter into his arms, kissing her on the cheek.

"Well, practice makes perfect, darling," he said, looking with awe at the governess. "And you are very fortunate to have such an incredible music teacher."

Miss Stewart blushed again, but there was a small, sweet smile too.

"I have a wonderful instructor," she said, shrugging modestly. "My aunt taught me that a deep love for music is the best teacher."

Cedric nodded slowly, enraptured with her speaking. Servant or not, he was finding it more and more pleasant to be in her company.

"Miss Stewart is by far the best governess I have ever had," Sophia said, turning to grin at her governess. "She is nice and smart, and every lesson is fun with her."

Something inside Cedric tore at his insides as his daughter spoke. He was grateful that Miss Stewart and Sophia got on so well. But this was the first time Sophia had expressly said that she had been unhappy with her other governesses.

Cedric knew, of course. He'd heard rumors spread amongst servants on occasion, and many of the former governesses had no reservations about telling him that his daughter's bi-colored eyes were repulsive.

He never understood how people could be so judgmental of his little Sophia. She was sweet and kind, as well as smart and clever. And those she loved, she did so with devotion and ferocity. It was rare that a child of noble birth in London was not spoiled and brattish. Sophia was an angel, and yet most people could not look past her physical differences.

No doubt the birthmark on the governess's face had contributed to the bond his daughter shared with the young woman. Sophia had at last found someone who truly understood the world through her eyes.

Cedric had always been understanding and patient about his daughter's eyes, but he could not empathize. Clearly, Miss Stewart could. And Cedric admitted that he could see many similarities in their personalities, no doubt because of their shared experience with cruel people. What Cedric could not understand was how the world could be so cruel and mean to two people who were so loving and compassionate.

"Papa," Sophia said, insistently enough to make Cedric realize she had spoken twice.

"Yes, darling?" he asked, trying his best to look attentive.

"I believe you are forgetting something," she said, glancing pointedly at Miss Stewart and then looking back at him.

Cedric looked at the governess, embarrassment taking hold. He had been so caught up in his thoughts, and with the spell her music had put on him, that he had forgotten a question of the utmost importance.

"How are you feeling, Miss Stewart?" he asked.

The young woman gave him another shy smile, and he felt his heart melt.

"I am much better," she said, her voice soft and as melodic as the notes she had just been playing. "I am not in any pain anymore, so I thought it prudent to return to Sophia's lessons immediately."

Cedric nodded, feeling awed. It was refreshing to see an employee so dedicated and passionate about their work.

"That is wonderful news," he said, truly meaning his words. "We have been quite concerned about you since your fall."

Miss Stewart nodded, her expression growing serious.

"It was only a minor tumble," she said. "But I want to thank you for what you have done for me. I understand that it is not orthodox for you to have cared for me in the way you have, and I want you to know that it is deeply appreciated."

Cedric's heart pounded. Her eyes were sincere, but there was sadness there. Did she think she had put him out in some way by helping her?

Before he could answer her, however, his mother entered the room. When she saw the governess and Sophia, she gave them a grand, bright smile.

"Oh, Miss Stewart," she said, gushing to the young woman. "It is wonderful to see you back at your post again."

Miss Steward blushed, rising to curtsey to her mistress.

"It is wonderful to be back, your ladyship," she said shyly. "I hardly knew what to do with myself while I was not teaching."

"And I could hardly stand not having my lessons," Sophia said, gazing fondly at her instructor.

The duchess smiled, nodding, and glancing at her son with approval.

"This is happy news," she said. "I do not mean to interrupt, but the garden tea party is about to start. The rest of the guests have arrived, and they will be looking for you."

Cedric felt his heart fall, even as he smiled at his mother.

"Very well," he said, facing Miss Stewart and his daughter once more. "Please, continue your lesson as long as you wish. The two of you play beautifully."

With heavy disappointment, Cedric turned and followed his mother out of the music room. He tried to prepare himself for the party as they made their way to the garden, but all he could think about was how he longed to return to the music room with his daughter and the governess.

"Miss Stewart has been a very good influence on Sophia, it seems," his mother said. "It has been ages since our dear Sophia has been so content and happy."

Cedric nodded, thinking dreamily of the joy he saw on his daughter's face any time she was with Miss Stewart. More amazing was that the joy was mirrored on the governess's face, as well.

"Indeed," he said, glancing over to see his mother smiling.

The duchess led him through the garden and along the path leading to the lawn where the party had been set up. She looked up at him just as the guests' voices reached their ears, and she gave him another, knowing smile.

"I believe that hiring Miss Stewart was decidedly the best decision we have ever made," she said.

Cedric looked at her, feeling his cheeks heat up as she looked at him. He did not know if she could guess his feelings for the governess, but he did his best to hide them.

"I couldn't agree more, Mother," he said, smiling. "I am glad that you convinced me to have faith in your decision to bring her into our employ."

The duchess reached out, taking her son gently by the arm. There was a question on her lips, and Cedric held his breath. Fortunately, she did not get the chance to ask whatever she intended.

A second later, Olivia appeared, walking with Lady Isabel and Edgar. When his friend saw them, he raised a hand, calling to them and beckoning them over to where the table stood.

Cedric grinned nervously at his mother, gesturing to the party waiting for them.

"Shall we, Mother?" he asked.

The duchess furrowed her brow, studying him a moment longer. Then, she shrugged.

"We shall, indeed," she said.

Chapter Twenty-three

Rosalie breathed deeply of the rich fresh air the instant she and Sophia stepped out into the gardens. Beth had been kind enough to open the window to her bedchambers whenever Rosalie had asked.

But even the gentle breezes that blew in could not compare to breathing the concentrated fragrances of all the roses and wildflowers that constituted the lovely gardens she had missed. But the fresh air brought more than sweet smells.

It brought with it the promise of a lovely afternoon outdoors with little Sophia, which she had missed even more.

Sophia slipped her hand into Rosalie's smiling sweetly up at her.

"Miss Stewart?" she asked, pointing past a rolling hill at the edge of her father's estate. "I would quite like to take a walk to the lake, just over there." She paused, glancing at Rosalie's feet. "That is, if you are sure that it would not be too much of a struggle for you."

Rosalie grinned. She was unaware there was a lake nearby. In an instant, she was envisioning herself sitting by the water, sketching away happily, with Sophia and Princess playing nearby.

"Of course, we can," she said.

Sophia giggled and nodded.

"Princess will enjoy chasing the dragonflies, I'm sure," she said.

As they walked, with Princess gamboling along beside them, Sophia talked excitedly about the music lesson they'd had that morning. But Rosalie quickly became distracted. She heard laughter coming from toward the front of the manor. She looked up and spotted a familiar man standing outside with an unfamiliar looking young woman.

Though she could not hear anything that was being said, she could see the woman was looking up at the duke with rapt attention. Jealousy surged through Rosalie, and she forced herself to look away.

How I wish I had not been born with this damnable birthmark, she thought, sadness and shame filling her heart. She did not think she could be compared to the diamond of the *ton* ever in her life. But she did feel sure she would have been considered pretty at least, if not for the hideous blemish that took up so much of her face.

She could not help that it was there, nor could she do anything to change it. It was unfair that everyone treated her like a criminal for it, and that she would never have a normal, happy life.

"Miss Stewart," Sophia said, her tone suddenly worried. "Are you all right?"

Rosalie looked down to see the girl staring up at her with wide, worried eyes. The girl cared dearly for her, and there she was, wallowing in self-pity. Many other women in her position were not as fortunate as she.

She had, after all, found two patient, kind employers, despite her hideous facial affliction. And now, she had a pupil who not only respected her, but seemed to genuinely love her. And Rosalie certainly reciprocated that love. She scolded herself for letting herself get stuck in such selfish thoughts, and gave the girl a true, sincere smile.

"I am all right, darling," she said. "I was in deep thought, but I am back now."

Sophia beamed again instantly, hugging Rosalie tightly.

"I am glad," she said.

A few moments later, they reached the lake. It was, indeed, small, but it was the most beautiful that Rosalie had ever seen. It overlooked the vast countryside, which was dotted with a great variety of wildflowers.

Sophia chose a spot amidst some beautiful yellow flowers and sat down, reaching for Princess with one hand and patting the ground beside her for Rosalie to join her.

"This is a very lovely place, Sophia," Rosalie marveled.

Sophia nodded smugly.

"I knew you would like it," she said, smiling.

They sat quietly for a moment, and Rosalie took in the scenery. It truly was the most magnificent sight she had ever beheld in nature; it wasn't a mere lake.

The sun reflected perfectly on the surface of the silvery water, making it appear clear and almost luminous; wildfowl skimmed across it, and bejeweled dragonflies performed their acrobatics in the hazy air; the summer breeze swayed the elegant rushes and tall yellow and purple flags, and was cool enough to make one feel perfectly comfortable as it blew in off the lake.

"Princess, no," Sophia said from beside Rosalie.

Rosalie looked up to see Sophia running after the pug, who had run off to chase after a host of butterflies. She could not help smiling as she rose, preparing to follow Sophia. However, her young pupil surprised her. She ran faster than ever, catching up to Princess quickly and grabbing her by the collar.

"Bad girl, Princess," she said, kissing the animal even as she admonished her. "Don't scare off the butterflies."

The dog was clearly not happy about being dragged away from her game. But when Sophia produced a piece of meat from her dress pocket and commanded the dog to lay beside her, the little pug complied.

"She is learning more every day, Sophia," Rosalie said, smiling fondly at the pair.

Sophia clasped her hands beneath her chin proudly.

"Just as I am," she said.

Rosalie nodded.

"Exactly like you," she said. "And speaking of learning, I think we should have our next art lesson right here. I can't quite believe we have never come here before."

Sophia suddenly grew serious and uncomfortable. She fiddled with some blades of grass in front of her, chewing on her bottom lip. Rosalie feared she had made the girl think she was angry. She was thinking of how to fix the issue when Sophia spoke again.

"I never thought for us to come here because I used to come here to hide from my previous governesses," she said, looking up at Rosalie. "But, since you came, I have not needed to come here. I had a dream about this spot last night, and it occurred to me that you might like it here as much as I do. Especially since you love to draw surrounded by nature."

Rosalie was touched by the little girl's words. She thought back to some of the things Sophia had said to her before, and she bit her lip, knowing the answer to her question before she even asked.

"Were all your previous governesses mean to you?" she asked.

Sophia looked at her with an expression far wiser and sadder than her eight years warranted.

"Yes," she said. "They all thought I looked wrong because of my eyes. They said mean things to me, and sometimes they made fun of me. It made me really sad."

Rosalie's eyes filled with tears, and she had to force herself to blink them away before the child saw them. She knew that pain all too well, and it broke her heart to know that grown people could be so horrible to a young child as wonderful as Sophia.

"Well, I have never thought anything about your eyes except how beautiful they are," she said.

Sophia nodded, her brilliant smile returning.

"I know," she said, wrapping her arms around Rosalie and squeezing tightly. "You are the very first governess to ever say so. In fact, I think you are the first person besides Papa to ever look past my appearance. Maybe that is because you are beautiful, just like me."

Rosalie was confused, but only for a moment. The girl planted a small, sweet kiss on her cheek, right on the birthmark. That was the first time anyone had ever called her beautiful besides her own father. Her heart swelled with love for the child, and fresh tears filled her eyes. She pulled the child back into her embrace to try to control her emotions.

At last, she pulled away from Sophia, giving her a sweet smile full of love and admiration.

"You most certainly are beautiful, darling," she said. "And you must remember that, always. Even when other people cannot see your beauty, you must never forget that it is there. You must never let anyone judge you by your appearance. After all, none of us can help the way that we are born. What truly matters is what is inside our hearts. That is who we truly are."

Sophia listened carefully as Rosalie spoke. Her expression was deep and thoughtful, and Rosalie thought again just how lovely her eyes truly were, especially when she was concentrating.

"Is that what helps you when people are mean to you?" she asked.

Rosalie considered pretending that people weren't really mean to her. But Sophia was too smart, and she would know better. Everyone in the manor had seen her birthmark, so there was no use in trying to act as though it was not there.

"Yes, it is," she said, mostly truthfully. "And I also try to remember that not everyone can understand. And people often fear what they don't understand. So, it is really no one's fault, so long as we remain true to who we really are inside."

Sophia nodded, hugging Rosalie once more.

"You are just as wise as you are pretty, Miss Stewart," she said.

Rosalie held her breath to suppress a sob of joy as she patted the girl on the back. But the sound of barking pierced through their tender moment.

Chapter Twenty-four

Cedric breathed a heavy sigh, looking around at the turnout for his mother's tea party, which was in full swing and had expanded to include games of Shuttlecock and Battledore. Of all the events they had hosted recently, Cedric thought the tea party guest list was second only to that of the ball a few nights prior.

He had spent several hours mingling with the guests as dutifully as he had at every other event. But his energy and patience were quickly depleting, and he wished the party would hurry up and end. With all the guests occupied in one form or another, Cedric saw another rare opportunity.

He casually sipped a glass of wine, slipping slowly through the clusters of guests until he reached the far outer entrance to the gardens. He surreptitiously sidled around the surrounding wall of shrubs, feeling instant relief as he moved farther away and the sounds of the tea party gradually died off, replaced by increasing peace and quiet.

Soon, all Cedric could hear was the song of the many birds flitting throughout the gardens and the trees of the wooded area at the back of his property.

He wished he could make for the stables and take a ride for a couple of hours. But his mother and sister would notice his absence, and so would all the guests.

So, instead, Cedric turned in the opposite direction and headed toward the small lake nearby.

Just as he topped the low hill not far from the lake, Cedric paused. There, just ahead of him, sat Miss Stewart and Sophia. He proceeded to move up behind them, intending to call out to them so as to not startle them if they should turn around and suddenly find him approaching. But before he could do so, he caught what they were saying, and he halted, his heart suddenly filled with pain.

To his horror, Sophia was explaining to Rosalie how mean and harsh all her former governesses had been to her. He knew of the one who had called Sophia "evil," but he had no idea that any of the other governesses had ever been anything more than uncomfortable near his daughter.

Overhearing that most of them had been downright cruel and had even berated her for her appearance shook his very soul. He clenched his jaw as tears filled his eyes. What kind of injustice had he done his daughter by not being more concerned with the way his employees treated her?

A shrill barking pierced the air, and Cedric stopped. The sound came from behind him, not ahead of him, as he had expected. He also noticed that he had not been spotted, as Sophia and her governess were no longer in sight.

Princess ran straight up to him a moment later, leaping up on her back legs but, instead of pouncing on his breeches, she slowly lowered herself back to the ground and sat, panting and trembling with excitement. Cedric laughed, surprised the little dog had not immediately jumped up on him, and he bent down to pet her. The puppy stood instantly, jumping up and down with joy.

He gently scooped up the dog, hoping that her continued barking would not mean he was discovered by his daughter and her governess. Then, they came into his sight again. As he got closer to the pair, he understood why his daughter had not immediately raced after her puppy and, thus, discovered his presence there.

"You must remember that Princess will never go too far away from the people she trusts," the governess was saying. "That means, if she is not within eyesight, then she has likely found your father or your grandmother, and she simply wishes to greet them.

Therefore, you do not need to endanger yourself by running away from me when she runs. You and I can go after her together, so then, you will be safe."

Cedric smiled at the loving guidance the governess was giving his daughter. There was no anger with his daughter's impulsive behavior. There was only patience and love, and Cedric was grateful. He realized that his mother had been right about Miss Stewart; she certainly was a blessing to his daughter. And, perhaps, to him, as well.

"Good day, ladies," he said, bending down to put a squirming Princess on the ground. "I believe I have found your escapee."

His daughter laughed, jumping up to run over and hug her father. The governess stood, giving him a very stiff, formal curtsey.

"Good day, Your Grace," she said, standing upright again.

Cedric dipped his head, patting Sophia on the back.

"And good day to you, Miss Stewart," he said. Then, he turned to kneel before his daughter and wink at her. "I trust your lessons went well today, as you are out here."

Sophia nodded; she was beaming, and Cedric noted that he had seldom seen her eyes sparkle so brightly.

"Miss Stewart says I shall be well versed in playing the pianoforte in no time," she said, grinning with pride.

Cedric looked at the governess, recalling how beautifully she had been playing when he'd discovered her with his daughter in the music room. He felt a slight shiver at the memory, which he masked by shifting his weight and dipping his head to the governess again.

"Well, in that case, I must attend some of your lessons," he said. "Let it not be said that your father did not show an interest in your rise to the status of pianoforte-playing prodigy."

Sophia clapped her hands and jumped up with excitement. Miss Stewart, however, had bright red cheeks. Every time she blushed, he thought about how endearing she looked. She lowered her gaze shyly, but Cedric could see her peeking up at him through her lashes.

Each time I think she cannot be more beautiful, she gets more beautiful, he thought, his breath catching in his throat.

"Papa," Sophia said, pulling at the sleeve of his jacket.

Cedric cleared his throat, reluctant to take his eyes off the lovely governess.

"Yes, Sophia?" he asked.

His daughter paused just long enough to take Miss Stewart's hand with her other one.

"Can we skip pebbles on the lake?" she asked, batting her eyes at him. "Please? Miss Stewart has taught me so much, and I would like to teach her something."

Cedric chuckled. He had taught Sophia how to skip rocks one day, a couple of years prior, when she was especially down about one of her governesses leaving. He realized it had been some time since he had come to skip rocks with her. Caught up in the emotions of the day and in feelings he had never felt before, he gave the governess a conspiratorial wink.

"Perhaps," he said, pretending to think hard for a moment. "But only on one condition."

Sophia looked at her father with wide eyes.

"What condition?" she asked.

He knelt in front of her, leaning forward, speaking in a low voice that would be just loud enough for the governess to hear.

"We must not tell your grandmother," he said, turning to Miss Stewart. "Will you keep our secret?"

The governess smiled fondly at Sophia, then looked back up at him. There was something of an impish glint in her eyes as she gave him her now familiar, heartwarming shy smile.

"Your secret is safe with me," she said, biting her lip.

Cedric took a breath and nodded.

"Then, I suppose it is settled," he said. "Would you like to join us, Miss Stewart?"

The young woman's cheeks turned pink again, and her eyes grew wide.

"I really know nothing about skipping rocks," she said. "I fear I would only make myself look foolish. Or, worse, that I might accidentally hurt one of you."

Cedric looked down at his daughter, who was bouncing with excitement.

"Well, since Sophia has offered to teach you, I suppose you could spend the day recalling what it feels like to be a pupil yourself," he said, grinning. "And we are not so fragile. A bump with a small pebble will hardly break us."

"No!" Sophia chimed in with enthusiasm. "It's really easy, Miss Stewart. Please, say that you will skip pebbles with us?"

The governess looked back and forth between Cedric and his daughter as though making sure the invitation was real. Her hesitation made Cedric's heart ache, and he gave her a reassuring nod.

"All right," she said, wearing her adorable bashful smile. "Thank you. I have always wanted to try skipping pebbles."

Sophia threw herself at the governess with such enthusiasm, the pair nearly fell over; they laughed as Cedric looked on with wonder. He could not recall a time when he had felt so carefree and happy, and seeing his daughter feeling the same way was healing to his soul. And he intended to savor every moment of it.

Chapter Twenty-five

Her heart pounding, Rosalie took the handful of flattish pebbles the duke had selected and now held out to her. She felt sure she should not have agreed to do something as fanciful as skip pebbles with her employer. What if someone were to see them? She could only imagine the gossip that might come of it. And what if Lady Olivia was the one to see them?

With a weak excuse on her lips, Rosalie prepared to hand over her pebbles to Sophia and flee from the lake. But the child was as intuitive as she was smart, and she was looking at Rosalie with wide, pleading eyes.

"Do not be afraid," she said. "I promise, it will be fun."

Rosalie stared at the little girl. Her mind was torn in two. It would be bad if someone discovered the three of them skipping stones together, to be sure, but how could she say no to Sophia, who was such a sweet and amazing child? It was such a simple, innocent request, after all

"All right," she said, tucking her pebbles into her apron pocket. "I will trust you to teach me well."

Sophia's face brightened once more, and she nodded.

"I shall not fail you, Miss Stewart," she said, grinning.

A few moments later, Rosalie stood beside Sophia, watching carefully as the girl skillfully tossed a couple of pebbles across the water to show Rosalie how it was done. Rosalie could feel the duke's eyes on her as he stood behind the pair, but she dared not glance back at him. She reminded herself that she was only there for Sophia, and that her behavior must be nothing but proper.

"Now, you try," Sophia said, moving back a couple of steps.

Rosalie brushed strands of hair out of her face and breathed deeply.

"I think I can do it," she said. "You have, indeed, been a very good teacher."

Sophia held her head high and gave Rosalie a smug smile.

"I concur," she said. "Let us see what you have learned."

Rosalie smiled, touched by Sophia's antics; she was imitating Rosalie's posture and using a similar tone of voice as the governess always did when teaching. Rosalie reached into her pocket and retrieved a smooth, flat stone. After carefully surveying the lake's surface, she tossed the pebble at the still water. Instantly, it sank, quickly disappearing from view.

"It is all right," Sophia said, giving her a wise, patient smile. "Try again. Next time, you will get it right. I believe in you."

But the girl was wrong. The second pebble sank faster still than the first, as did the third, fourth and fifth. Rosalie's cheeks flushed with embarrassment, and she looked at her young tutor sheepishly.

"It looks as though I will never get it right," she said.

Sophia gave her a stern but affectionate look.

"Do not be silly," she said. "You are smart and talented. You just need more practice. Practice makes perfect, after all."

Rosalie's heart swelled at the child's encouragement. It did not matter to Rosalie if she never perfected skipping pebbles. The moment they were sharing just then was more important to her than anything else in the world.

"Here," the duke said softly, approaching Rosalie with a kind smile. "Perhaps I can assist you. There is a simpler way to hold the pebbles as you skip them, but it will be easier for me to show you."

Before Rosalie could respond, the duke stepped up behind her. He reached for her hand, placing a pebble in her palm. Then, he turned the back of her hand with the tips of his fingers until her hand was completely flat. He gently rotated her wrist so that it was perfectly straight, not taking his eyes off hers.

Rosalie felt she might swoon. The scent of his sandalwood cologne was heady, and his soft touch set her blood on fire. Butterflies flitted around in her stomach as he guided her on how to stand, placing his other hand on her upper back. When he stepped away from her, she felt an instant sense of loss. She could not help noticing that he, too, looked a bit flushed, and perhaps even a little disappointed.

"Now, watch me," he said, his voice husky and deep. Rosalie shivered, nodding as he took the same stance he had shown her. He tossed the pebble with the greatest of ease, and it skipped easily and quickly across the water.

"Try for yourself," he said with encouragement.

Rosalie took a deep breath, trying to steady herself. She made sure the pebble rested in her hand just the way the duke had shown her. She closed her eyes, envisioning the way the duke had tossed the pebble.

Then, she opened her eyes, throwing the stone just as the duke had taught her. To her surprise, it skimmed across the top of the lake just as his and Sophia's had. The duke and his daughter both began applauding vigorously.

The young girl squealed with delight, embracing her governess tightly.

"I knew you could do it, Miss Stewart," she said, squeezing.

125

The duke cheered gleefully.

"That was a marvelous throw, indeed," he said, still clapping. "In just a few rounds, you will have perfected pebble skipping, I do declare."

Rosalie looked at him shyly, blushing furiously as he smiled at her. She knew it was wrong, but she could not help allowing herself to revel in his gaze. Her skin tingled, and her body felt hot, and she slowly returned his smile. His lips looked so soft, and suddenly, all she wanted in the world was to kiss them.

"Toss another, Miss Stewart," Sophia said, jumping up and down. "Skip one with me."

Rosalie giggled, breaking her gaze from the duke, and looking down at the excited little girl. She pulled out another pebble from her pocket and prepared to skip it, just as she had the previous one. But the sound of voices froze Rosalie in her place.

With horror, Rosalie looked up to see Lady Olivia approaching from just over the hill. And she was not alone. The two people Rosalie had encountered the day she twisted her ankle accompanied her, and they were all staring with at the trio standing by the lake.

Rosalie stiffened, and her stomach twisted into knots. It was too late to flee, and likely too late to fumble for an excuse as to why she was so casually lingering with the duke and his daughter. She bit her lip, uncertain as to what would come next, too afraid to even glance at the duke.

"Cedric," Lady Olivia said sharply, not taking her eyes off the governess. "What are you doing down here, by the lake?"

The rest of her question lingered, unvoiced, but Rosalie saw it clearly in her piercing glare. She tried to swallow, but she found her mouth was incredibly dry. She shifted her weight uncomfortably and looked away from the duke's sister. But she could still feel the daggers shooting from the young woman's eyes.

There was a long, awkward moment of silence. Rosalie could not bear the tension, so she knelt and busied herself with emptying the stones from her dress pocket. She did not dare look back to see if Lady Olivia was still watching. If the burning sensation on the back of her head was any indication, she most assuredly was.

"Cedric," the young woman said again, attempting to veil the hostility in her voice that time. "We were wondering where you had disappeared to. Several of the guests have been asking for you. I expected to find Sophia down here. It is lucky, I suppose, that we found you, as well."

Rosalie dared to look from the corner of her vision in the direction of the duke. Lady Olivia was still too far behind to see her clearly, but the duke looked like a disappointed child. He sighed, looking right at Rosalie for the briefest of moments before turning back to his sister.

"Do not worry yourself, Sister," he said. "I simply wanted to have a little fun with my daughter. I was unaware that she was here with Miss Stewart, however. Sophia and I were just engaging in a little pebble skipping."

Only then did Rosalie dare to stand. The duke had not mentioned that she had also been skipping pebbles with them, for which Rosalie was relieved. But deep down, she knew that Lady Olivia had seen her with her own pebble in her hand, and that she was well aware that Rosalie had joined in with them.

Olivia nodded, her smile false and her eyes suspicious. Fortunately, however, she did not press the subject.

"Well, come," she said, reaching toward her brother as though he had offered her his arm. "We shall accompany you back to the manor."

The duke hesitated. He looked at his sister for a long moment, and Rosalie wondered if he would dismiss her.

Rosalie looked away, pretending not to take note of the other two people standing with Lady Olivia. The young man was watching with mild interest. But the woman beside him, who bore a striking resemblance to him, had her gaze fixed directly on the duke.

Rosalie's heart fell as she studied the woman, who was looking at the duke as though he was responsible for placing every star in the night sky. It was clear to her that the young woman had some feelings for the duke, and she herself had absolutely no right to expect anything at all from him.

Still, as she stared between the duke and the woman, she felt a surge of jealousy. She knew Lady Olivia was largely responsible for the interruption. But it could not be denied that the other young woman had an interest in the duke. Nor could Rosalie deny any longer to herself that she had feelings for him, as well. But what was the best she could expect from the scenario unfolding before her?

As she admired the young woman's beauty, the duke cleared his throat. Rosalie tried to turn her full attention to him, unable to ignore the way the other woman gazed at him affectionately. Her heart sank, but she tried to focus only on the duke, and whatever was about to come from his lips.

"Very well," he said after a long moment of silence. "I would not wish to keep our guests waiting any longer."

Rosalie's heart fell as he turned back to her and Sophia. He gave them a wan smile as he bowed formally.

"Please, forgive me," he said, looking at Rosalie with an expression that she was sure was forlorn and unhappy. "I must take my leave. I wish the two of you a wonderful day."

Sophia ran toward her father, taking one of his hands in hers.

"Oh, Papa, can't you stay?" she asked.

The duke shook his head, smiling sadly at his daughter.

"I must go, darling," he said, kissing her forehead. "I want you to be good for Miss Stewart."

As he spoke her name, the duke looked at her. For a moment, it appeared as though his expression was sad and apologetic. But then, he bowed, and his face became solemn and expressionless, and Rosalie's heart sank.

"I bid the two of you a wonderful afternoon," he said, turning away before either of them could say a word.

Silently, she and Sophia watched as the duke walked away, joining his sister and their friends as they headed back toward the manor. Right then, Rosalie realized she did not belong in the duke's world. Any attraction she thought she felt between them must be hers alone; there was no possibility that he could ever consider her an equal.

"Miss Stewart," Sophia said, tugging on her dress. "Does this mean we must go inside?"

Rosalie looked down at the child, trying to consider her answer carefully. The duke had clearly left the day up to her, and she did not wish to let the girl know how upset she was. From then on, her only concern was to ensure she was a good governess.

"No, darling," she said, smiling. "We can stay here as long as you wish."

Chapter Twenty-six

It was all Cedric could do to not look over his shoulder as he allowed the trio to lead him back toward the mansion. He was completely oblivious to all conversation around him. He knew he had duties as lord of the manor, especially if his guests were asking after him.

However, the only thing he truly wished to do was return to the lakeside and spend the rest of the day with his daughter. And, he admitted, the beautiful governess.

"Cedric," Olivia scolded, snapping him out of his daze. "Have you been listening to a word I've said?"

Cedric nodded, searching his mind for any indication he had accidentally picked up on anything she'd been saying.

"Of course," he said. "You were telling me about which of the guests have been asking for me."

Olivia stopped walking and rolled her eyes.

"No," she said, shaking her head. "I have spoken with Isabel and Lord Burtondale, and they wish to go horseback riding with us tomorrow morning."

Cedric flinched. From the edge of his vision, he could see that Lady Isabel and Edgar had stopped to look curiously at Cedric and Olivia, no doubt having heard her voice rise. Embarrassed, he looked at this sister and gave her a curt nod. He began walking forward again, trying to ignore the grin on his friend's face.

Olivia huffed, stomping ahead of him as she glared at him over her shoulder.

"I shall see to all the arrangements," she said. "I do hope that you can pull your head from the clouds by then."

With that, Olivia caught up to Lady Isabel. Cedric took a moment to wonder at his sister's sudden interest in befriending Edgar's sister. When they had first arrived, Olivia had seemed to hardly acknowledge Lady Isabel's existence.

Edgar slowed to wait for Cedric to catch up to him. He was still grinning as he patted Cedric on the back.

"It appears as though we each have sisters underfoot," he said. "What delirious fun it has turned out to be, chaperoning them."

Cedric rolled his eyes, praying that Olivia did not see.

"I need a drink after my dear sister's outburst," he said.

Edgar laughed.

"What was that about, anyway?" he asked. "If her eyes had been daggers, you would be a dead man, my friend."

Cedric shrugged. He knew it, of course. He did not, however, wish to discuss why he had been so lost in thought that he had not heard his sister speaking to him.

"To embarrass me in front of you and your sister, I suppose," he said.

Edgar snorted.

"It does sound as though she is ready for marriage," he teased.

Cedric joined him in a chuckle. *I am certainly ready for her to marry,* he thought to himself.

As they made their way inside the manor, Cedric realized something that almost made him curse aloud. Olivia had led them to the mansion, not to the garden, where the party had been held. He also realized that he could not hear the sounds of guests in or near the rooms in which they had been hosting their social events.

That meant that his sister had made up the story about guests asking for him, knowing well that they were gone, and that none would be returning until that evening. Why she should do such a thing was beyond him. He only knew that it made him quite agitated. He could not understand his sister's strange behavior as of late. Hopefully, she would soon find a suitor and her temperament would improve.

The sound of Olivia's musical laughter made him look at her once again. Not for the first time, her whole mood had taken a complete opposite turn. She was talking with Cedric's friends as though she had not a care in the world.

Specifically, Edgar. Cedric watched for a moment with a bemused smirk. *If I didn't know better, I would think that my dear sister has a crush on the illustrious viscount.*

Cedric shook off the thought just as quickly as it crossed his mind. He knew well that Edgar was not seeking to settle down any time soon. And he knew that Olivia was seeking a genuine match who was seeking a wife.

Surely, what was happening between Olivia and his best friend was simply the playful budding of a friendship. And if Olivia did have other thoughts in mind, Cedric believed that Edgar would kindly explain his intentions to her without hurting her. Or, at the very least, Edgar would speak privately with Cedric and allow him to handle it, if his friend was too afraid of hurting Olivia's feelings.

"I suppose the guests got tired of waiting for me," Cedric jested, giving his sister a look that told her he knew what she had done but had no intention of embarrassing her over it. "Olivia, would you like to take tea with Lady Isabel?"

Olivia looked at Edgar almost longingly, making Cedric second guess his earlier assessment. Then, she looked at Lady Isabel, giving her a wan smile.

"That would be lovely," she said, her voice again changing and sounding less than thrilled.

Cedric turned to Edgar and smiled.

"Would you join me in the parlor for a drink?" he asked.

Edgar nodded enthusiastically.

"I thought you would never ask," he said.

With Cedric leading the way, he and Edgar made their way to the parlor. Cedric had one of the servants fetch his scotch and two glasses while he and his friend made themselves comfortable on the sofa. The drapes were pulled away from the tall windows, giving the room plenty of light.

When the drinks were poured, Cedric raised his glass to his friend with a wry smile.

"To getting our sisters successfully matched this Season," he said cheerfully.

Edgar nodded, growing thoughtful as he clinked his glass to Cedric's. The two men shared a sip in silence before Edgar spoke.

"That is actually something about which I wish to speak with you, Cedric," he said, slowly setting his glass on the table before them.

Cedric choked on his drink, washing it down with another before putting aside his glass. Was Edgar about to confirm his suspicions about whatever was happening between him and Olivia?

"Oh?" Cedric asked, his voice cracking. He cleared his throat, trying to swallow down the scotch that lingered while he collected his thoughts. If that was what his friend was about to say to him, he wanted to be prepared.

Edgar raised an eyebrow quizzically at Cedric, then nodded.

"I am well aware that you wish to see Lady Olivia at least on her way to being married by the end of this Season," he said. "And I have the same wishes for my own sister."

Cedric nodded, taking another long, but much slower, drink of his scotch.

"Yes," he said, momentarily confused. "Hence why I chose those specific words for the toast we just shared." He paused, deciding it would be best to just get what he was sure Edgar was about to say out in the open, before it drove him mad. "What is it that you wish to say to me?"

Both he and Edgar looked surprised. Cedric had not intended to sound so tense and worried, but clearly, they both noticed it.

Edgar leaned forward, his eyes kind but his expression very serious, almost nervous. Cedric held his breath, waiting for what felt like an age.

"I wish to ask if you would consider a courtship with Isabel," he said.

The breath Cedric had been holding whooshed out of him, and he looked dumbly at his friend. He knew he had not misunderstood the suggestion, but it was the last thing he'd expected Edgar to say.

"Oh," Cedric said dumbly. He picked up his glass, deliberately taking a big drink from it. He had no idea what to say to such a sudden proposition, but he knew he must tread lightly.

"I know it must seem a bit sudden," Edgar continued, "but I have noticed that you and Isabel have been spending more time together. And it appears that my sister has taken quite a liking to you."

Cedric nodded, avoiding his friend's gaze. He could never tell Edgar that he had only been spending time with his sister because he knew it was expected of him. Nor could he tell his friend that he had no interest in his sister. How, then, could he deal with the situation in which he suddenly found himself?

"That is quite an offer you have put before me," he said, choosing each word with the utmost of care. "What on earth made you consider saying such a thing?"

Edgar smiled, temporarily relieving Cedric.

"Well, as I said, it is clear to me that my sister has an interest in you," he said. "And I wish her to make a match with a gentleman who is not just suitable, but also genuine and honorable. And, if any gentleman in the *ton* is those things, it is you, my friend."

Cedric swallowed, hiding behind his glass. His friend of so many years had just become a perfect stranger. He did not know how to respond to the proposition; he must choose his next words very carefully.

"Your sister is a very lovely young lady," he began.

Edgar nodded, grinning proudly, waiting for Cedric to continue.

"She is, indeed," he boasted. "Any man of the *ton* would be lucky to have her. And I do not presume to speak for her, but I do hope that you might be the first to vie for her affections."

Cedric finished his glass, wasting no time in pouring another for both himself and his friend. What on earth could he say that would not sound offensive? It seemed ironic that he should be considering such a thing, given that Edgar himself was not one for thinking of settling down and looking to marry. But he knew it was hardly the moment to bring that up.

"You propose something great, indeed, Edgar," he said as he finished pouring the drinks. "I hope you will not think me too cowardly if I ask you for time to consider your proposition."

Edgar's eyes widened, and he nodded knowingly.

"Oh, of course," he said wisely. "What kind of brother would I be if I did not allow a prospective suitor time to consider such a proposal?"

Cedric nodded, relieved, but also concerned. What kind of friend needed time to consider such a proposal? He knew Edgar likely had a different impression of the amount of time Cedric had been spending with Lady Isabel than was actually the case. But simply to accept his friend's suggestion was beyond Cedric at that moment.

For another hour, he and Edgar talked of business ideas and plans for the future. But not for a moment did Cedric forget what his friend had said to him. He knew well that Lady Isabel would make a fine and proper wife for him. But he could not picture himself married to her. How could he ever express such thoughts to his friend, especially now that Edgar had given him such a direct proposition?

Chapter Twenty-seven

The following morning, Rosalie's first thoughts upon waking were of the duke. She'd had such a wonderful time with him and little Sophia before his friends and sister had discovered them by the lake and called the duke back to his party.

And she would never forget the way that her entire body had tingled when the duke had put his arms around her to show her how to properly skip the pebbles. He was handsome, to be sure, and she felt an attraction to him the like of which she had never felt before toward any man.

With a sigh, she forced herself from her bed. It would do her no good to entertain such thoughts about the duke. He would never see her as anything more than his daughter's governess. And why should he? He was nobility, and she was merely his employee. He would probably think it laughable to learn that she felt anything more for him.

In truth, she could hardly blame the duke. He was as attractive as he was kind, and he likely had more wealth than Rosalie would ever see, even if she lived ten lifetimes. He deserved an attractive, refined wife, much like the young woman with Lady Olivia and Lord Burtondale the day before.

Certainly, he would never prefer a woman like her, not when a woman so lovely and noble looked at him as though he had already captured her heart. With a heavy heart, she dressed and made her way to the servant's kitchen for breakfast.

Beth was notably absent, so she sat alone, as far from the other servants as she could get, to eat her meal. Naturally, without Beth to intervene or distract her, she became acutely aware that the other staff huddled together, ceasing their loud, merry conversation in favor of hushed voices and whispered tones.

She wanted to ignore them and pretend they were having no effect on her. That was hard enough to do when they sat around, making no effort to hide the fact that they were whispering about her. But then, Irene stuck her head up from the cluster of murmuring servants, glowering at her with pure hatred and disdain.

Succumbing to the discomfort, she turned her chair around. She supposed she could not blame them. Who would ever wish to be associated with someone as beastly as her?

I would, she thought as she forced herself to finish her now cold porridge. *I would never judge someone based solely on their appearance.* She thought back to what Sophia had said about her previous governesses. If the servants were so cruel and mean to her, were they also this horrible to Sophia?

After breakfast, Rosalie hurried from the kitchen, ignoring the titters of laughter that followed her out of the room. She made her way toward the schoolroom, looking forward to Sophia's lessons, as she always did. Spending time with the child always made her happy, even after such cruel treatment from her peers.

Just as she passed Sophia's bedchambers, which she noticed with no surprise was empty, Lady Olivia stepped into view. Rosalie's heart filled with dread, but she forced herself to curtsey to the young woman.

"Excuse me," she said, hoping to simply keep walking past the angry young woman. "I cannot be late for Miss Sophia's lessons."

Lady Olivia sneered, deliberately stepping in front of Rosalie so that she could not pass.

"This will only take a moment," she said. "And it likely will not matter anyway. You will be done here after I have spoken my piece."

Rosalie swallowed hard.

"Done?" she asked nervously. "What do you mean?"

The young woman clearly relished Rosalie's discomfort. Her cold smile sharpened, and she narrowed her eyes at the young governess.

"You do not belong in our world," she said, gloating. "And since you do not seem to realize it, I must be the one to tell you. It brings me no great joy, of course, but it must be said."

Rosalie could see that it did indeed bring her joy. And it did not take Rosalie long to understand what she meant. She was referring to the afternoon before, when she had been caught with the duke and Sophia by the lake.

"I can assure you..." Rosalie began, but the young woman put up her hand so fast and so close to Rosalie's face, she thought the woman might slap her.

"I can assure *you* that whatever impression you are under is the wrong one," she said. "Our dear Cedric is too kind for his own good. He has pity for the afflicted of society such as you. Unfortunately, it almost cost him dearly, and it is because of you."

Rosalie's eyes widened. Had her misguided judgment gotten the duke in some kind of trouble?

"I would never wish that, of course," she said quickly, trying to keep the young woman from interrupting her again. "Whatever has happened, I will stand and ensure that everyone knows it is my fault, not his."

Lady Olivia frowned, her upper lip curling up into another sneer.

"Of course, it is, you ninny," she hissed, glaring at Rosalie. "I had to do a great deal of convincing to get the guests who accompanied me yesterday and discovered you cozying up to my brother and niece to promise to keep silent about what they had seen. I am sure I do not need to tell you what would happen if rumors of *that* incident got around."

Rosalie's heart dropped. She had known it was a bad idea to allow herself to become so familiar with the noble family for which she worked. But she had not thought the duke's own sister would be the one to expose such an affair.

"They will keep silent," Lady Olivia continued, clearly not caring about any response from Rosalie. "But surely, you do not need reminding of the damage it would do to our family should the *ton* to find out about you *skipping pebbles* with Cedric."

Rosalie felt a mixture of horror at her worst fears being confirmed and anger at the gall of Lady Olivia. Rosalie would never admit that the duke had insisted she join them, as it would only serve to further harm his reputation.

But for his sister to assume that her brother would simply allow her to force her presence on himself and his daughter was insulting. She had no right to speak to Rosalie in such a manner.

"If you are concerned that I shall tell someone, I can assure you that I shall not," she said. "Now, I do not wish to be rude, but I really must see to Miss Sophia's lessons."

But once again, when Rosalie tried to step around the young woman, she blocked her path.

"You are not understanding, little governess," she hissed, putting her hands on her hips. "So, I will phrase it in a way that even you can understand. You jeopardize us all by being here, especially after that little display. And if our guests were to learn that you still work here, I am not certain that I could once again convince them to keep quiet. It would be best for everyone if you packed your bags and left." She smirked before adding her final words on the subject. "Especially for little Sophia's sake."

Before Rosalie could gather herself to respond, Lady Olivia sneered one last time and stormed off, leaving Rosalie alone in the hallway. Rosalie shook her head in disbelief, replaying the young woman's words unbidden . Had her reckless actions truly jeopardized not only the reputation of her employers but of Sophia, as well? Had Lady Olivia simply been trying to be cruel to her, or was she right about what she had said?

Struggling to compose herself, Rosalie made her way to the schoolroom. She knew that no matter what the case, she must push her emotions aside for the sake of Sophia. Even if Lady Olivia had a point, she could not allow the child to see that she was upset, or that such a distressing conversation had taken place.

Sophia was not present when she entered the schoolroom. Rosalie frowned, but she was glad to have a moment to collect herself before the young girl arrived. She did not know what she would do beyond that day, but she knew she could not make it Sophia's problem.

Still, she could not help wondering where Sophia was. The child was normally there before Rosalie arrived. Perhaps she had overslept and was getting dressed at that very moment.

Rosalie paced around the room, looking around at all the materials she had used in the past weeks. The duke had provided the best learning materials for his daughter, and she had learned well. But Rosalie had noticed that Sophia had learned the most from putting her lessons to practical use outside the schoolroom.

With a sigh, Rosalie began to draw on the blackboard. She did not know what was keeping Sophia, but she hoped her pupil would arrive soon. She did not know how much longer she could dwell in her own thoughts.

She wanted to believe that Lady Olivia was wrong in her assumptions, and in her cold advice that Rosalie's leaving would be for the best. But the longer Sophia remained absent, the more Rosalie began to think that maybe the duke's sister might be correct.

With a heaviness unlike any she had ever experienced, Rosalie at last collapsed into her seat at the head of the room. She knew little of the life of nobility, but she knew enough to stay out of it. But what she could not make sense of was what Lady Olivia had said to her.

She knew by experience that Sophia loved her dearly, and that the child had dealt with terrible people in her life. Was it possible that Lady Olivia was just blissfully unaware of the hell that her niece had been through with other governesses? Did the young woman truly think she was helping Sophia?

Whatever had prompted Lady Olivia to confront her so directly, Rosalie decided that it could not be selflessness. She herself was a flawless, beautiful young woman.

There was no possibility she could understand how it felt to be shunned by Society. Therefore, nor could she imagine that her own niece knew how it felt to be treated in the way Rosalie herself was often treated.

At least, Rosalie had to believe that. To entertain the idea that Lady Olivia knew what her niece went through yet could still be so cold was inconceivable to her. If the young woman was right about her needing to leave the family, Rosalie knew it would be up to her to figure out how to tell Sophia. Surely, a lady born of nobility would not misguide her, at least, not about something as important as the future of an impressionable young girl.

"Rosalie," came a voice from the open door of the schoolroom.

Rosalie started, realizing she had been staring at the desk and tracing an outline of London on the map spread out across her desk.

"Yes?" she asked, looking up at a very flustered Irene Jennings.

The young woman looked frantically around the room, staring in disbelief at Rosalie.

"Sophia is not with you," she said, more a statement than a question.

Rosalie shook her head, alarm rising within her.

"No, she is not," she said. "She is not with you?"

Irene shook her head, looking at Rosalie with something other than disdain for the first time since Rosalie had met her.

"No, Rosalie," she said, her voice cracking. "Miss Sophia has gone missing."

Chapter Twenty-eight

Cedric was happy to let Lady Isabel, Edgar, and Olivia ride ahead of him as they wound along the paths in the forest behind Livinwood Manor.

He kept up pleasant responses and vague murmurs when someone shouted back to him, but he was not focused at all on anything the trio ahead was saying.

Rather, his mind was on the previous day, when Edgar had proposed that Cedric court Lady Isabel. He had no doubt Edgar would soon invite him for drinks to get an answer. It was an answer which Cedric did not have.

He was certain Lady Isabel would make a good wife. So, why did he hesitate to take Edgar up on the offer?

He sighed, allowing himself to catch up a little to the rest of his party. Over the past several days, it had become clear that his little Sophia needed a mother figure. And, although they had never discussed it, Cedric felt sure Lady Isabel would be a kind, doting mother to his daughter. Still, as hard as he tried, he could not imagine his and his daughter's life with her in it.

Instead, he kept envisioning Miss Stewart's smiling face. There was no denying the connection and affection between his daughter and her governess. And he had to admit that Sophia had never been happier or more outgoing than she had since Miss Stewart began teaching her.

But it was more than that: He could no longer deny he had developed strong feelings for the young woman. And he knew it was that which was truly preventing him from accepting his friend's offer.

"Cedric, if we ride any more slowly, we will be at a standstill," his sister teased, fluttering her eyes flirtatiously at Edgar as she spoke. "Will you be catching up with us anytime soon?"

Cedric made a face at her, nudging his horse forward quickly toward hers, so close that it made her squeal.

"Is that enough for you, Sister?" he asked.

Edgar and his sister laughed. Cedric did not fail to spot that Lady Isabel was looking at him in much the same way that his sister was looking at his friend, but it was nothing compared to the bashful, innocent way Miss Stewart smiled at him.

Olivia glared at him before turning her attention back to Edgar and saying something he did not care to hear. Cedric thought he would like some more peace and quiet.

Suddenly, Edgar and Olivia moved a good bit further ahead on the trail, still within sight but well out of earshot, and Lady Isabel fell behind. Another moment later and he drew level with Edgar's sister.

She smiled uncomfortably at him, glancing toward her brother, and rolling her eyes.

"How lovely of them to leave us behind in such a way," she said. "Although I do believe that my brother has taken quite a liking to your sister."

Cedric smiled wryly, choosing not to respond. He was still positive that Edgar had no intentions of settling down. He just hoped he was right, and that his friend would not break his sister's heart.

"They would not make such a terrible couple," he said, half teasing. "But I sometimes wonder if my sister is ready to settle down herself. She has seemed to enjoy her Seasons so far without finding a match."

Cedric winced inwardly, afraid he had said something untoward. But Lady Isabel simply looked at the pair ahead of them as though pondering something.

"I do not know," she said thoughtfully. "Perhaps she has simply taken a genuine interest in my brother, and she hopes he will pursue her."

Cedric opened his mouth to voice his previous thoughts, but he closed it again. Was he wrong about the interactions between them? And was any interest his sister might feel for Edgar reciprocated?

Before he knew it, he was lagging again. This time, it was Edgar who noticed it first, turning his horse in the middle of the trail and looking at Cedric with bemusement.

"If I didn't know better, I would swear we are riding with an old man," he said.

Cedric narrowed his eyes, a smirk twitching on his lips.

"Perhaps you three would be interested in a race back to the stables, since you think I am so slow," he said, not looking back. With a laugh, he spurred his horse and guided it in the direction of the trail that would take them back to the stables.

Behind him, he heard the shouts of his companions as they kicked up their horses and picked up speed. He set aside his strained earlier thoughts for that moment to enjoy the good-spirited race.

Just before they reached the stables, Cedric saw a blurred figure running away from the manor. He brought his horse to a stop just in time to see it was the governess.

She was running toward the lake with a speed that astounded him. He only saw her face for the briefest of seconds, but that was all it took for him to see that something was terribly wrong.

He hurriedly dismounted his horse, preparing to ask Edgar to return it to the stables. But before he could take another step, his sister had brought her mare to a halt directly in front of him and leapt off, standing before him with her hands on her hips.

"Where are you off to?" she asked, frowning. "I have arranged for us to picnic together for lunch. It would be rather rude of you to run off now."

Cedric looked at his sister, entertaining the notion of having a debate with her. But he glanced back, watching the way the governess rushed past them without a trace of acknowledgement. Something was very wrong indeed, and he knew he should investigate.

"Dear Sister," he said, "please, go on and start without me. I shall join you as soon as I can. I must take care of something rather important first."

Before she could protest, Cedric turned away from his sister and ran after the governess, who had already vanished from view.

By the time he reached the lake's edge, Cedric's chest ached, and he was terribly out of breath. He stopped to put his hands on his knees and look around for the frantic governess. There was no sign of her at first, and he began to wonder if he had been imagining things. When he finally spotted the young woman, however, his heart dropped into his stomach.

Miss Stewart's face was pale and, even from where he stood, he could see tears streaming down her cheeks. She was soaked from head to toe, her dark hair clinging to her face and shoulders. He felt bile rise in his throat when he saw she was carrying his daughter out of the lake, unmoving, and paler than the governess, in her arms. *No,* he thought, racing over to the woman. *Please, God, no...*

He rushed over to them, reaching them just as Miss Stewart collapsed to the ground on her knees.

"I am sorry," the governess said as he took Sophia from her. "I am so sorry, your lordship."

Cedric looked at her as he cradled his child to his chest. He opened his mouth to speak, but no words would come.

"Please, forgive me," Miss Stewart spoke again. "I did not know. I was going to the schoolroom to begin her lessons. She ran away without anyone knowing. It is my fault. I am so sorry."

Cedric shook his head, holding his still, freezing daughter close to him.

"Is she breathing?" he asked, gently lowering his daughter to the ground.

The governess shook her head, putting her face in her hands.

"I do not know, Your Grace," she said. "I ran out here as soon as I heard she was missing." She succumbed to her tears, sobbing wildly for a moment. "Please, forgive me."

The duke's heart broke. He had no idea what had happened, but he knew the governess was not to blame. His only concern was his daughter, and whether she still lived.

Trembling, Cedric put his hand up to his daughter's mouth. No breath touched his skin, and his heart began to pound wildly. He moved his shaking fingers to Sophia's throat, holding his breath and praying. He choked out a sob as he realized that, though weak, his daughter had a pulse.

"She is alive," he croaked, gently lifting the girl once more. As he did so, she began to cough up water. The governess rushed over, tilting her head so that the water would fall from her blue lips and not get sucked back down her throat. When the coughing ceased, however, the girl fell unconscious once more.

"We must get her back to the manor," Cedric said, fueled by fear and numb with shock simultaneously. "Now."

Chapter Twenty-nine

The taste of blood made Cedric cease chewing on his bottom lip. He did not stop pacing, however. Every moment that passed while the physician was in his daughter's bedchambers was an eternity of agony for Cedric. He had never even considered that he could outlive his child. But now he faced that very possibility, he felt his soul being ripped to shreds.

Though he tried, he could not hear any indication that his daughter had roused from the unconscious state in which he and Miss Stewart had found her. He felt sure that hell could not be as bad as what he was feeling in those moments.

What could have made so careless? Cedric wondered, trying to make sense of what had happened. Sophia spent a great deal of time outdoors, and he knew she loved the lake. But she had never gone into the water without supervision. Why had she suddenly do so that day?

"Darling," his mother said, taking him gently by his shoulders. "Would you like me to stay with you?"

He stopped his pacing at last, looking at the duchess. Her whole face was stained with tears that she had clearly attempted vainly to wipe away. For a moment, he wished he was a young boy again, so he could fall into his mother's arms and let her soothe the ache in his heart.

"No," he said weakly, shaking his head. "You should go and see the guests and apologize to them for such an abrupt ending to the festivities."

His mother bit her lip, fresh tears slipping down her cheeks. Cedric took a handkerchief from his jacket pocket and handed it to her, trying his best to look braver than he felt. He was no young boy anymore. It was now his duty to comfort his mother, despite the utter fear he felt.

"Everything will be fine," he said, clearing his throat to mask the lump of emotion that had formed in his throat. "Go and bid everyone farewell. I promise that I will come and fetch you as soon as I speak with the physician."

The duchess nodded at last.

"Very well," she said, caressing Cedric's cheek. "I love you, darling."

"I love you too, Mother," he said, clenching his jaw to suppress his own tears.

He watched his mother disappear down the hallway, then resumed his pacing. *What can be taking so long?* he thought, wringing his hands. *Please, God, let her be all right. I cannot lose my little Sophia.*

He recalled the moment when Miss Stewart had stepped out of the lake with his limp daughter in her arms. She had looked as frightened as he felt, and he felt guilty for having sent her away when the physician had arrived. He promised himself that he would go out of his way to show his gratitude to the governess for rescuing his daughter. He only prayed that the rescue had not come too late.

"Your Grace?" said a soft voice from behind him.

Cedric whirled around, rushing over to the physician before he had even shut Sophia's door behind him.

"Is she all right?" he asked, frantically grabbing the doctor's shoulders. "Please, tell me that my daughter is all right."

The physician put comforting hands on Cedric's shoulders. His eyes looked tired, but behind the fatigue there was a hint of a warm smile.

"She will make a full recovery, Your Grace," he said.

Cedric felt his knees buckle, and suddenly he realized why the doctor had grabbed hold of his arms. The man steadied Cedric, letting the duke lean on him until his legs ceased their trembling.

"Thank you, Doctor," he said, his voice as shaky as his body. "I will be forever in your debt."

The physician shook his head gently.

"Being able to give you such good news is its own reward," he said. "Now, little Sophia will need to rest for a couple of days, and I will come and check in on her, to be sure there is no fluid lingering in her lungs. But I believe the water has already made its way out. She was very fortunate, indeed, to be found when she was."

Cedric gripped the physician's hand in both of his, squeezing perhaps a bit too hard as he shook it.

"Thank you again," he said hoarsely. "Thank you."

The physician nodded, stepping aside, and gesturing toward Sophia's door. Cedric bid him a good day, then entered the room.

To his relief, Sophia was conscious, sitting up in bed holding her dog. Her skin was slowly returning to a semblance of a normal color, and her lips were once again pink. She was in dry clothes and wrapped up in several blankets, no doubt to combat any chill she might have got in the water. But, most importantly, she was alive. Cedric closed his eyes, squeezing them tightly to fight against his tears.

"Darling," he said when he trusted himself to speak, "I am so glad that you are all right."

Sophia's lip began to tremble, and Cedric rushed to her side. He held her for a moment, sure that the surge of emotion came from having had such a close call. He kissed her still damp hair over and over, sending up prayers of gratitude to the heavens.

"It is all right," he whispered, holding his daughter close to him. "Papa is here, sweetheart. You are going to be all right."

She mumbled something Cedric could not hear, and he looked down. Sheepishly, he pulled back, realizing that, in his fit of gratitude, he had squashed her face against his chest.

"Forgive me, Sophia darling," he said. "What did you say?"

"Where is Miss Stewart?" she asked, sounding as though her throat was sore and clogged.

Cedric gave his daughter a tight smile.

"I imagine she is in the servant's quarters," he said. "You must rest now. I am sure that she will come and see you when she can." He could not tell his daughter that he had made her governess go away. He did not wish to further upset her.

Instead of calming, however, she only began to cry harder. Cedric could hear a faint rattle in her chest, but otherwise, her breathing seemed clear and unobstructed. Cedric held his daughter, thinking she was still suffering from the shock she had experienced.

When at last Sophia's sobs did subside, he pulled away gently, just enough to look down at his daughter's tear-streaked face.

"Darling," he said, asking the question he was unable to resist asking any longer, "why did you do that? Why did you run into the lake that way?"

Sophia sniffled, holding Princess tightly to her, but for a long moment she did not respond. During her hesitation, Cedric wondered if he should not have waited to confront his daughter until she'd had some rest. But the longer the question hung unanswered in the air, the worse the knot of dread in his stomach grew.

"Papa?" Sophia asked at last, looking up at him with pleading eyes. "Please, do not send Miss Stewart away. Please!"

Cedric's mouth fell open. Her plea caught him so off guard that it was now he who was without words. In her state of unconsciousness, could she have overheard him ask the governess to go and wait elsewhere while the physician examined her? Was it that which had upset the child?

"Sophia, sweetheart, I only asked her to go downstairs and wait until I could speak with the doctor," he explained.

Sophia shook her head hard enough to make her neck pop. She looked at Cedric with fresh tears pouring down her face.

"No, Papa," she said. "I overheard Aunt Olivia tell Miss Stewart that she should pack her bags and leave. She said really mean things to her and said that Miss Stewart was putting us all at risk with the *ton* by staying here."

She began to sob once more, but she continued speaking.

"That is why I ran to the lake. I did not mean to fall in. I was running too fast to stop and I fell. I was afraid that you would send her away and find another mean governess, so I was just trying to hide away. But now that she's rescued me, you can't send her away, can you?"

Cedric felt his blood boil. It was all he could do to keep his temper in check. He'd known all along how uncomfortable Olivia was with the governess in the house; she had expressed as much quite clearly. But to be so horrible as to go behind his back and tell the young woman she should leave, when she knew Sophia cared so deeply for her, infuriated Cedric.

"Papa?" Sophia asked, looking at him with worry. "Are you angry with me?"

Cedric threw his arms around his daughter once more, realizing then that he was trembling.

"Not at all, sweetheart," he said, kissing her all over the top of her head once more. "I am not angry with you at all. I am glad that you are all right. And Miss Stewart is not going anywhere. I promise you that, darling."

Sophia's face instantly flooded with relief. She returned her father's hug, squeezing hard.

"Thank you, Papa," she said. "I love you."

Cedric rose, patting his daughter on the head.

"I love you more than anything, Sophia," he said. "I will come to check on you again a little later. But I must go and take care of something important first."

Sophia nodded, smiling, and cooing to her puppy. Cedric left the room, still struggling to contain his anger. He stormed away from his daughter's room on a mission: He would find his sister. And he would speak with her.

Storming through the manor, Cedric called for his sister. When she appeared from their mother's parlor, he grabbed her by the arm. She looked as though she wanted to protest, until he glowered at her as he pulled her along. He brought her into his study, slamming the door before he dared to speak to her.

"What the hell do you think you were doing?" he asked, glaring at his sister.

Olivia donned a mask of pure innocence.

"What is wrong, Brother?" she asked.

Cedric tried to compose himself, suppressing his trembling as he spoke.

"You told the governess to leave," he said simply.

Olivia tried to feign innocence.

"I do not understand," she said, but Cedric held up his hand. Truthfully, he wished to slam his hand down on the desk nearby, but it would serve no purpose.

"You told Rosalie to leave our home," he said through clenched teeth. "Do not pretend to be ignorant of the matter. You told her to leave, and you put Sophia in direct peril."

Olivia's eyes widened, and he knew he had his sister's attention. He waited for an explanation, but none ever came.

"Do you know what has happened?" he demanded.

Olivia studied his face for a moment, eventually shaking her head.

"I do not," she said, her expression turning from defiant to confused.

Cedric stepped away from his sister, shaking his head.

"Sophia nearly drowned," he said. "She ran away after hearing you so cruelly lecture the governess."

Olivia paled. She stared at her brother for a long moment, shaking her head slowly.

"Cedric, you must believe me—" she began. But Cedric shook his head, holding up his hands and stepping away from his sister.

"Do you understand that Sophia could have died?" he asked, glaring at Olivia.

His sister's face fell, and he saw tears fill her eyes.

"I would never wish harm to Sophia," she said weakly. "I adore her."

Cedric could not help but snort as he stared at his sister.

"Then explain to me why my daughter threw herself into the lake after overhearing a conversation between you and the governess," he hissed.

Olivia grew paler still. She reached out for Cedric, who stepped back, slapping her hands away.

"I am sorry that Sophia heard Miss Stewart," she said.

Before she could say more, Cedric grabbed his sister by the shoulders.

"I know what was said, Sister," he hissed. "Do not pretend that you did not instigate the conversation. I want to know what the hell came over you.'

Olivia's lip trembled.

"Is Sophia all right?" she asked.

Cedric frowned, eventually nodding.

"She will be fine," he said. "Not that it is of any consequence to you. You would send away the only employee who has cared about her, and why?"

Olivia shook her head, looking surprisingly stunned and shamed.

"I would never wish to see Sophia harmed," she said, her voice pleading. "How could I know that she would put herself in harm's way?"

Cedric sneered at his sister, shaking his head.

"You know nothing about your own niece," he said, turning to leave the room. "Keep yourself out of my sight.

Chapter Thirty

Rosalie did her best to suppress her worry for Sophia as she hurriedly changed out of her wet clothes. She knew what she had to do after speaking with Olivia, but all she could think of was the little girl. How could she even consider leaving when she had no idea if Sophia would recover?

The horrific image of seeing Sophia floating face down in the lake flooded her mind. Her heart began to race again, just as it had when she'd reached the water's edge.

The child had appeared to be trying weakly to flail her limbs when Rosalie first spotted her. By the time she had reached Sophia, she had stopped moving altogether.

When she had looked down at the young girl's pale face and blue lips, she had been certain it was too late. It was pure adrenaline that allowed Rosalie to wade out of the lake and put the girl in her father's arms.

She had been numb with terror and sadness, and she felt as though her world was crashing down around her. How could she have allowed such a thing to happen in the first place?

It was only when the duke had said the child had a pulse that Rosalie had been able to pull herself out of her shocked state and help him get her to the manor. She only hoped that Sophia would fully recover.

She would never be able to forgive herself if Sophia did not survive. Even though she had made up her mind to leave, she would make sure that the sweet girl was all right before she left.

She packed her things as quickly as she could, trying to shove away thoughts of Sophia. That the girl had been coughing up water when they got her to the manor was a good sign. As she put her belongings in her trunk, Rosalie tried to believe that Sophia would be all right,

She knew she could never force herself to leave if she believed anything else. It was an impossible thing she was about to do. But Lady Olivia had made it abundantly clear that she must leave. And surely, after what had happened with Sophia, the family would want her gone. As much as she would miss the little girl, perhaps it would be best for everyone. Everyone, that was, except for her.

Just as she reached for the last of the items she needed to pack, she found the sketch book Sophia had given her. As if in a cruel twist of fate, it was turned to the page where she had sketched Sophia and Princess.

A vice clamped around her heart as she studied the page. She knew she would miss them terribly, and she hurriedly closed the book as her unshed tears began to fall.

A knock at the door caused her to jump out of her skin. She turned, brushing wildly at her wet cheeks, to see Beth standing in the doorway of her chambers.

"Rosalie," Beth said, her brow furrowing. "The duchess has asked to see you. Are you all right?"

Rosalie nodded, even as her tears poured down her cheeks.

"I shall go to the duchess straightaway," she said, turning her face away from her friend.

Beth was not having any of it, however. She approached Rosalie, putting a soft hand on her shoulder.

"Whatever is troubling you, you can tell me," she said. "If there is something I can do to help you, you know I will be happy to do so."

Rosalie looked at her friend for what she knew would likely be the last time. She fell into her arms, sobbing, as the housekeeper patted her back gently.

"I believe that today will be my last day here, Beth," she said when she could speak.

Beth looked at her as though she had gone mad, shaking her head in disbelief.

"Why, Rosalie?" she asked. "You do not think the family blames you for what happened to Miss Sophia, do you?"

Rosalie shook her head, not knowing what to say. The duke had been sharp in dismissing her when the physician had arrived, but he was a father who was in fear for his child's life. She did not truly believe that he blamed her for the accident.

However, she also knew that she should not speak a word about what had taken place with Lady Olivia. She wiped at her face furiously, making up her mind to speak further with the housekeeper before she left.

"I should not keep the duchess waiting," she said. "I will come and find you later, and we can talk."

Beth looked dissatisfied with the answer, but she simply nodded.

"Very well," she said. "Do not fret, Rosalie. I am sure that everything will be fine."

But as Rosalie made her way down the stairs, she began to worry more still. Perhaps the duchess blamed her, even if the duke did not, and had she sent for her to terminate her employment. At least, if that was the case, she would not need to explain anything further to Beth.

And perhaps she would not feel so bad about leaving. She certainly blamed herself for Sophia running away. She should have gotten to the schoolroom sooner. She should have pushed past Lady Olivia and dealt with any repercussions afterward. Anything would have been better than letting Sophia hurt herself. Or worse.

With her stomach in knots, Rosalie made her way to the drawing room. The door was open, perhaps in anticipation of her arrival, and inside sat a very distraught and worried looking duchess. Rosalie's heart broke as she entered the room, and the lady of the manor met her eyes.

"Rosalie, please," she said, motioning the governess over.

Rosalie complied, trying to push aside her own worries and fears to comfort the duchess.

"Your ladyship," she said with a curtsey. "How is Sophia? Is she all right?"

The duchess's lip quivered, and she dabbed at her eyes with the twisted handkerchief she held.

"I am waiting for Cedric to speak with the physician," she said. "I believe she will be all right, though. Which is why I wished to speak with you."

Rosalie swallowed, but she gave her best smile.

"Of course, my lady," she said.

The duchess nodded, taking a big, shaky breath.

"You were so brave in going to our little Sophia's rescue," she said, choking on a sob. "I cannot allow myself to think of what would have happened had you been a single minute later. You did precisely what I would expect from you, going after her immediately. And you put yourself in peril to save her. And for that, Cedric and I will be forever in your debt."

Rosalie's stomach twisted. She was relieved that the duchess did not blame her for the accident. But now, she was reluctant to tell the duchess that she intended to resign. All she wanted to do was embrace the lady of the manor and wait with her for the duke to tell them how Sophia was.

"You owe me nothing, Lady Livinwood," she said. "I am so glad that I reached Sophia in time. I love her very dearly, my lady." She paused, taking a breath. "Which is why it pains me to tell you that I must resign. You and the duke have been wonderful to me, and Sophia is the best and sweetest little girl in the world. But I must leave, Lady Livinwood."

The duchess looked horrified. She rose from her seat, reaching out and taking Rosalie's hands.

"Oh, dear," she said. "If I have put too much pressure on you about having saved Sophia, I apologize. Rest assured that I am grateful to you, but I would never make it your responsibility alone to keep her safe and healthy."

Rosalie shook her head, her tears falling.

"No, it is not that at all," she said. "I just feel that it is time for me to leave. You are all wonderful, and I love you all. But I do not think I should remain here anymore."

"You are not going anywhere, Rosalie," thundered the duke from the doorway. The two women jumped as the duke rushed into the room. His hair was wild, and his eyes were wide and red, and Rosalie's heart fell into her stomach.

"Darling, is she all right?" the duchess asked.

Her son looked as though he did not understand her question, staring at Rosalie for a long moment before speaking.

"Yes, Mother," he said quickly with a curt nod. "Thank the heavens, she will be fine." He stepped toward Rosalie, still not looking at his mother as he did so. "And you, Rosalie, will *not* be leaving us."

Rosalie's heart raced between the beats it was skipping. Could he know about the conversation between her and his sister? Or was he just reacting to overhearing what she had just said.

He took a breath to calm himself, looking at his mother. He gave her a small, but warm, smile.

"Mother, Sophia is all right," he repeated. "But would you mind giving Miss Stewart and me a moment alone? I will explain everything later. But first, I owe her an explanation, and an apology."

The duchess looked at the two, nodding at last. Reluctantly, she left the room, but not before quickly hugging Rosalie.

"Thank you again, dear," she said.

Rosalie watched as she left the room. Then, she turned to the duke, who was watching her with his ever-intense gaze.

"Your Grace," she began.

To her surprise, the duke held up his hands, shaking his head.

"Rosalie, you needn't explain a single thing," he said. "I spoke with Sophia, and she told me why she ran out to the lake."

Rosalie nodded, unsure of what she should say. Even though she did not know why the girl had done such a thing, she did not wish to get the little girl in trouble.

"I do not understand," she said at last, desperate to get to the point of what the duke was trying to say.

The duke wiped at his face, and only then did Rosalie notice that he was crying.

"Sophia told me what my sister said to you," he said. "And I wish to set straight a few things right now. Sophia adores you, which I am sure you already know. But what you cannot know is that I do, too."

Rosalie gasped, stepping back. But the duke grabbed her hands, looking at her with wide, emotion-filled eyes.

'I adore you, as well, Rosalie," he said.

Rosalie covered her mouth with one hand, but only momentarily. The duke reached up quickly and took her hand from her face, giving her a subtle shake of his head.

"I understand that what my sister said to you was cold and cruel," he said. "But I would speak to you honestly and openly, if you would hear it."

Rosalie hesitated only briefly before nodding slowly. She wished to speak, but no words would come to her lips.

The duke nodded.

"I understand that this likely comes as a surprise to you," he said, "but over the past several weeks, I have come to admire your spirit. My Sophia loves you, and I can see why. And after your actions today, I can more than see why she loves you." He paused, reaching up and caressing the birthmark on her cheek. "I have also seen just how beautiful you are, and I believe you should understand that. But most of all," he said, kneeling down before her on one knee, "I think you should know that I have fallen madly in love with you."

Rosalie felt as though her knees might collapse. She fell, grateful for the stool she quickly realized was right behind her.

"Your Grace," she breathed, but the duke put a finger up to her lips.

"I will spend the rest of my life listening to every word you have to say to me," he said. "But you must promise me that you will agree to be my wife."

Rosalie was overwhelmed with emotion. She bit the inside of her cheek to ensure she was not dreaming. She had spent many nights wishing that the duke might feel the same way for her that she did for him. Now he was confessing exactly that, it was difficult for her to believe.

"Is there a chance that you are saying these things to me because I have just saved your daughter's life?" she asked, kicking herself for questioning her employer, and the love of her life.

The duke smiled sweetly at her, shaking his head softly.

"I understand why you might think such a thing," he said. "But only after learning that I might lose you, I realized I must tell you what I have been thinking since the very first moment I met you. Nothing will do for me in this life but to have you as my wife. I implore you to say yes, Rosalie. Because I love you more than life itself."

Rosalie felt as though she might swoon, but she found herself immediately in the duke's arms. She smiled up at him, just as she had in so many dreams. She was speechless, but only momentarily. She might never get another chance to confess her true feelings, and she did not intend to miss out.

"I am in love with you, too," she whispered. "Yes, Cedric. I will gladly be your wife."

Her fiancé lifted her so that their noses touched.

"I love you, Rosalie Stewart," he said, kissing her passionately.

Epilogue

"Is it true?" Sophia shrieked, bursting into Rosalie's bedchambers.

Rosalie turned, her face already brightening even before she met the girl's eyes. She did not need to ask what the child meant by her question. She understood what Sophia was asking.

"Yes, darling," she said, kneeling and opening her arms to the little girl. "It is true. Is that all right with you, Sophia?"

The child's mouth fell open, and she stared at Rosalie for a moment. Rosalie's heart pounded fiercely in her chest. She knew that Sophia adored her, as she did Sophia. But what if she had hoped that her father would marry a refined noblewoman rather than a mere governess?

Before Rosalie could blink, the child flew into her arms, nearly toppling them both to the ground. It had only been a day since Sophia's horrible accident, but the little girl already seemed to be good as new, for which Rosalie was ceaselessly thankful.

"Surely, you jest," she said, burying her face in Rosalie's neck. "This is the most wonderful news ever. You will be the best mother in the whole world."

Rosalie giggled, wrapping her arms tightly around the little girl.

"I certainly promise to work hard to be the mother you deserve," she said.

Sophia pulled back, looking at Rosalie with affection and admiration.

"Can I call you Mother?" she asked.

Rosalie put a hand on her chest. She was overwhelmed with emotion, and with her own love for the child.

"If you like," she said, blinking back tears of joy.

"Sophia, darling," the duchess said from the doorway of Rosalie's room, startling both of them.

The girl whirled around, clinging to Rosalie's hand as she looked at her grandmother.

"I know I should be in bed," she said, gazing happily at Rosalie. "But I was just so excited that I had to come see Miss Stewart first."

Lady Livinwood walked in, patting her granddaughter on the head softly. Then, she looked up at Rosalie and smiled.

"You certainly should be convalescing, little one," she said, reaching for Rosalie. "But seeing as this is such a special occasion, I suppose we can make one little exception, for just a little while."

Rosalie reflexively started to curtsey rather than take the elder woman's hand. But the duchess grasped hers, shaking her head gently.

"No future daughter-in-law of mine shall curtsey to me," she said, pulling Rosalie into an embrace. "I am truly honored to know that you will be part of our family."

Rosalie stepped back, smiling shyly at the duchess.

"I must say that it is an adjustment," she said. "Being not of noble blood puts me at a disadvantage. I know nothing of being nobility, let alone a duchess, your ladyship."

Lady Livinwood shook her head again, touching Rosalie's cheek.

"From now on, you may call me Dorothy," she said. "And do not fret. I shall help you with every part of your transition." She paused, glancing around the room. "Beginning immediately, with getting you out of here and moving you upstairs, to a bedchamber befitting a future duchess."

Rosalie blushed. It was the first time she had really considered how much her life would change now she was engaged to a duke and destined to become a duchess.

"That is kind of you, my ... Dorothy," she said. "But you needn't go to such trouble for me. I will be all right in here until Cedric and I are married."

The duchess shook her head, waving her hand gently.

"Nonsense," she said. "As far as I am concerned, you are already family. It is high time you were treated as such."

Sophia began cheering, and she threw one of her arms around each of the two women.

"This is the happiest day of my life," she said.

A knock on the door distracted them all once more. Beth stood outside, her eyes filled with excitement as she smiled at Rosalie. She curtseyed respectfully to the duchess before quickly embracing Rosalie. Then, she stood back, clearing her throat and smoothing out her apron.

"Pardon my enthusiasm, my lady," she said sheepishly to the duchess. "If you like, I can oversee having Rosalie moved upstairs."

The duchess smiled warmly at Beth and nodded.

"You are quite right, Beth," she said. "And yes, please see to it that Rosalie's belongings are taken upstairs, and then help her settle in once everything is in order."

Beth curtseyed again, stepping outside to summon another maid. Then, the two women set about gathering Rosalie's belongings, while the former governess stared in wonder.

"Come, Sophia, darling," the duchess said, putting her arm around the girl, who had just begun rubbing her eyes. "I shall tuck you in tonight. You really must rest, so that you can recover quickly."

"But I want to stay with Rosalie," she insisted, yawning as she spoke.

Rosalie leaned down and kissed her head softly.

"I promise to come and fetch you first thing in the morning," she said. "But your grandmother is right. Lots of rest will help you get well faster, so we can play outside again all the sooner."

Sophia nodded, seeming too tired to continue arguing.

"First thing in the morning," she murmured, echoing Rosalie. "I will not forget."

Rosalie smiled fondly as the duchess led the child from the room. When they were out of sight, Rosalie turned to face Beth, who was staring at her with big eyes.

"Oh, Rosalie," she said, rushing over to give her a hug. "I could not be happier for you."

Rosalie laughed, nearly suffocating in the housekeeper's tight grasp.

"What a turn of events this has been," she said, feeling overwhelmed.

Beth pulled away, tears of happiness in her eyes.

"I can think of no one more deserving than you, Rosalie," she said. "Um, I mean, Her Grace, Lady Livinwood."

Rosalie smiled at the sound of her future title, but she gave her friend a gentle shake of her head.

"I do not care if I were to become queen," she said. "I insist that you always call me Rosalie. You were my friend when no one else would consider such a thing. And you will always be my dearest friend."

Beth wiped at the tears that flowed down her cheeks.

"Well, now, I am even gladder that I chose to be your friend," she said, winking. "It will do my reputation amongst the staff a world of good to be friends with the new duchess."

The two women laughed.

***

The following month was simultaneously the happiest and longest of Rosalie's life. To maintain propriety, Cedric had returned to his family's London home, where he would remain until after they were wed. The Dowager Lady Livinwood did just as she had promised, spending much of her time everyday teaching Rosalie what she needed to know to become a proper duchess. She even took Rosalie shopping and bought her a wardrobe to last her well into the next year.

Sophia had chosen to stay with Rosalie and her grandmother rather than go to London with her father. Rosalie had insisted that she continue giving Sophia lessons, at least until after the wedding, when she officially became the Duchess of Livinwood. And they still ended their lessons each day by spending time in the gardens.

Sophia had, understandably, been reluctant to return to her spot by the lake. But a week before the wedding, she woke Rosalie early, begging to skip the day's lessons so they could spend the day there. Thrilled that Sophia was ready to conquer her fear, Rosalie had agreed. She had hurriedly dressed before Beth came in to help her, and they went outside.

They spent that day sketching and painting pictures of the lake. But just before they ended the day, Sophia climbed onto Rosalie's lap.

"Will you splash water from the lake in my face, Mother?" she asked.

Rosalie stared at the child, bewildered.

"Why?" she asked. "I cannot imagine doing such a thing to you, darling."

Sophia took Rosalie's face in both her hands.

"Because I do not want to be afraid of water anymore," she said.

Rosalie's lip trembled with emotion at the young girl's bravery. She was grateful to have the chance to be her stepmother. She knew there was a lot she could learn from the child.

"Very well," she said, with great reluctance. "But you must tell me if you get frightened. I do not wish to harm you, Sophia."

Sophia nodded, smiling sweetly.

"I know you would never hurt me," she said. "Besides, I wish to be brave and strong, like you."

Rosalie's heart swelled. She gently took the girl's hand and led her to the edge of the lake.

"Are you ready?" she asked, her hands shaking.

Sophia nodded, taking a slow, deep breath.

"I am ready," she said.

With gentle hands, Rosalie reached down, scooping up water and splashing it into the girl's face. Sophie gasped, wiping the water out of her eyes, and blowing it away from her lips. Then, she took another breath and giggled.

"Thank you, Mother," she said, sticking her hands into the water and grinning impishly. "Now, it is your turn."

***

The day when Rosalie married Cedric was the happiest of her entire life. They had both agreed that Sophia should stand with them during the ceremony despite the unorthodoxy of the situation. They felt it was a great way to show all of London that they were officially a family, and that the love they shared for one another was just as important as their marriage to each other.

The wedding took place at their country home, where they would reside as husband and wife. Cedric's friend, Lord Burtondale, attended, as did the dowager duchess. Even Olivia was present, having returned from Bath just two days before the wedding. It was a lovely, intimate ceremony, and Rosalie felt more joy in her heart than she could ever remember.

The dowager duchess hosted the wedding breakfast in the garden of the countryseat. Some of her friends and some of Cedric's business partners attended the party, as well as Beth. Rosalie felt it was only right that her best friend be allowed to share in the celebration of her special day.

Moments before the orchestra was due to begin playing the first tune of the day, Olivia approached the newlyweds. She hugged her brother, turning to Rosalie and giving her a small smile.

"May I speak with you in private?" she asked.

Cedric frowned, clearly wishing to protest.

Rosalie kissed her new husband on the nose, giving him a look of sincere intent.

"I shall return shortly, my love," she said.

Cedric hesitated for a moment before nodding.

"I shall be right here if you need me," he said, not taking his eyes off his sister.

Rosalie took Olivia's arm and led her to the end of the refreshment table. She did not know what to expect, but she felt that the least she could do was afford her new sister-in-law her time.

Olivia bit her lip and sighed.

"I was terrible to you," she said, far more bluntly than Rosalie could have anticipated. "Perhaps I have no right to ask this of you so soon, but I am truly hoping that you can eventually find it in your heart to forgive me."

Rosalie stared at the young woman. She knew Olivia had spent the past month at a seminary school in Bath, giving her plenty of time to think about her past behavior. But Rosalie sensed the apology and plea for forgiveness came from a place deeper than any school could teach. She embraced Olivia, thrilled the young woman had seen the error of her ways.

"Of course, I forgive you," Rosalie said. "Now, please, enjoy yourself. This is a celebration, and you are a very important part of it."

Extended Epilogue

A year and half after one of the happiest days of Cedric's life, he once more stood in front of the mirror in his bedchambers, dressing in his finest suit for yet another happy occasion. His valet smoothed his shoulders, giving him a knowing smile.

"I have only seen you grin so proudly twice before, Your Grace," he said.

Cedric wagged his eyebrows at his reflection, his smile widening.

"I hope you can grow accustomed to it, Benjamin," he said. "It is a look I expect to wear now for the rest of my days."

With that, he patted the valet's arm, thanking him briefly. Then, he went downstairs, where his beautiful wife awaited him before they left for the church.

When they arrived, he kissed his wife on the cheek, then sought out the bride. When he reached her, his heart swelled with pride and love.

"Sister, dear, you look absolutely beautiful," he said, kissing her softly on the cheek.

Their mother stood beside her, wiping tears of joy from her cheeks.

"Both of my darlings will soon be married," she said, hugging them both. "This is every mother's dearest wish."

Both Cedric and Olivia returned their mother's embrace. Then, the duchess excused herself to find her seat at the front of the church.

Cedric turned to his sister and smiled.

"Are you ready, Sister?" he asked, holding out his arm.

Olivia beamed at him, and Cedric knew he had never seen her so happy.

"I absolutely am, Brother," she said.

Cedric held up his head proudly as he walked his sister to the altar. He gave her without reluctance to Edgar. Before he took his place behind Edgar, he leaned toward his old friend's ear.

"One might think that you could not be happier right now, Edgar," he said.

His friend stuck out his chin.

"Whatever gave you that idea, Cedric?" he asked, his eyes shining.

***

In the weeks following seeing his sister married, Cedric found he only grew happier by the day. He arranged to do most of his important business from home or right in London. After the birth of his son, whom they had named Albert after Rosalie's father, Cedric wanted to spend as much time with his family as he could, and as little time overseas as possible.

Sophia took on her new role as a big sister with gusto and great love for her little brother. She spent every free moment with the toddler, tending to him with more dedication than even the new nursemaid did. Cedric had been puzzled when Miss Jennings had resigned shortly after he and Rosalie had married. But when Rosalie and Sophia explained to him how cruel she had been, to both Rosalie and Sophia, Cedric was glad.

The new nursemaid was older, but she was jolly, friendly, and kind. She had a big scar that ran along her left jawline, and Sophia and Rosalie adored her. As she did them. And the nursemaid, whose name was Brenda, simply worshipped little Albert. At last, Cedric knew he needn't worry about anyone being cruel to his family. He understood that he would forever be grateful for whatever force had brought Rosalie into his life.

One day, Cedric pulled Sophia aside, asking her to keep Rosalie busy outdoors while he slipped off to town. Sophia seemed to understand at once, running off to do exactly as her father had asked. He spent most of the day in west London, but he managed to find everything he sought.

After dinner that evening, Cedric once again pulled Sophia away from her stepmother.

"Go with Miss Brenda and keep your brother occupied until bedtime, my darling," he said.

Sophia nodded.

"You are giving Mother a surprise," she said knowingly. "May I see what it is?"

Cedric nodded, gently caressing his daughter's chin.

"You may tomorrow," he said. "I am certain that Rosalie will be thrilled to show it to you."

Sophia nodded, thrilled to have such a big responsibility before her. She hurried up the stairs to find the nursemaid and her little brother.

"Rosalie, darling," he called as his wife stepped out of the dining room. "Would you join me in your parlor, please?"

Rosalie looked at him quizzically, but she nodded, following him to her parlor.

Cedric waited for her to enter the room first, holding his breath. The instant his wife gasped, he knew she had seen it.

"Oh, Cedric, darling," she said as he slowly entered the room. "What is all this?"

Cedric glanced around at the easels, canvases, paints, and charcoals arranged carefully about the room. He had spent weeks choosing the best quality art supplies from all over the world, and he had paid the servants bonuses to haul it all in earlier that day and arrange it just the way he believed his wife would like it.

"I do hope you do not mind that it takes up the whole room," he said. "I noticed you hardly used this room as it was, and I also recalled that you are a very talented artist. I only apOlogize for not doing this sooner for you."

Rosalie turned to him, tears streaming down her cheeks and her smile bright. She ran to him, leaping into his arms and kissing his cheeks with vigor.

"You are the best husband in all of London, darling," she said. "But there is one problem."

Cedric looked at his wife with wide eyes.

"What?" he asked.

Rosalie giggled.

"Now, Sophia and I will never leave this room," she said.

***

For little Albert's second birthday, Cedric and Rosalie decided to host a small house party. Olivia and Edgar, who were just returning from their six-month-long wedding trip, happily accepted the invitation to attend. Lady Isabel and her husband, Lord Dwayne Kent, Duke of Kennington, would also be present. And, of course, the dowager duchess would be there, as well. She doted on Albert every bit as much as she always had on Sophia. She was just helping Beth finish all the arrangements as the first of their guests arrived.

Everyone filed out into the garden, enthusiastic about the picnic. Cedric greeted everyone with gusto, thrilled to have all the people who meant the most to him at his home. Once upon a time, he would not have believed he could be so happy. But knowing that he was made him feel as though he could rule the world.

The picnic was set up shortly after the guests arrived. Everyone was happy to do something to help, and before long they were ready to enjoy their meal. The smiles and pleasant exchanges were enough to fill Cedric's heart with love and joy, and he held his head up with pride.

"Excuse me, everyone," Edgar said, rising to his feet, before taking Olivia's hand and helping her to hers. "I do hope that this will not be an unwelcome interruption, this being young Albert's special day. However, Olivia and I would like to make an announcement, if we may?"

Cedric looked at Rosalie, who nodded eagerly.

"Say on, Edgar," he said, giving a nod of encouragement.

Edgar and Olivia shared a sweet kiss. Then, it was Olivia's turn to speak.

"We wanted all of you to be the first to know that very soon, Edgar and I shall be joining my dear brother and lovely sister-in-law in the blissful chapter of life known as parenthood," she said, glowing.

Cedric leapt to his feet, giving Edgar a hearty handshake, while Rosalie went over to Olivia and embraced her. The dowager duchess joined her daughter and daughter-in-law in their joyous embrace, delighted at knowing she would soon have her third grandchild.

Sophia joined her family, having picked up her little brother and put him on her hip.

"Might I nominate myself to be the new baby's nursemaid?" she asked. "I do very well with Albert and I do love looking after children."

Edgar and Olivia exchanged a look with one another. Then, Olivia looked at Rosalie, giving her a fond smile. When she turned back to her niece, she knelt, brushing a strand of hair out of her beautifully unique eyes.

"You are a bit young to be a nursemaid, dear," she said. "But you may certainly look after the baby whenever we come to visit."

Sophia, whose face had begun to darken at being told she was too young, suddenly smiled.

"Very well," she said. "And I shall be the best nursemaid in all of London."

Everyone laughed.

"I, too, am with child," Isabel said, almost too quietly for everyone to hear.

Her husband looked at her with surprise, kissing her softly on the cheek and chuckling.

"I did not know we were about to announce out happy news too," he said, gazing at his wife with adoration. "But since my darling wife has chosen to do so, then I can confirm with great pride that I, too, shall soon be a father."

Olivia shrieked, running over to Isabel, who had since become her closest friend apart from Rosalie, and embracing her tightly.

"You mean that we shall be with child together?" she asked excitedly.

Isabel nodded with excitement.

"Perhaps we shall give birth on the same day," she said.

The party continued, with everyone laughing and enjoying themselves. The dowager duchess's tears of joy continued all through the picnic, gushing over her young grandson and the grandchild who would soon be born. Cedric sat back, content to be amongst family and friends, relishing every laugh and smile.

Rosalie laughed, and he turned to see Sophia and Albert chasing a butterfly. Princess sat back, watching the pair with her head tilted, as though trying to understand the appeal of such an activity. Cedric, too, laughed as he recalled the little dog's past adventures doing precisely the same thing.

With a heart filled with love and joy, Cedric pulled his wife close to him. She leaned in willingly as he kissed her cheek, nestling her head into his neck as she sighed.

"Today is a most wonderful day," she said, her contentment warming his heart in a delicious way.

"It is, indeed," he murmured against the top of her head. "I hope you know that I fall more in love with you every single day."

Rosalie looked at him with mock surprise, batting her eyelashes.

"Why, Your Grace, whatever would your wife think of such a declaration?" she asked, giggling as she spoke.

Cedric leaned down, kissing his wife passionately on the lips.

"I hope she feels the same way," he said. "Because nothing would make me happier than to continue sharing such days with her, for the rest of our lives."